SKULL

Steel Patriots MC

Book 10

Mary Kennedy

Contents

CHAPTER ONE

"What do you mean you left college?" snarled Matt Crawford.

Scott watched as his father stood from the big leather recliner, stretching to his full height of six-foot-four, only one inch shy of his own height. Yet somehow, that one inch seemed inconsequential. Matt Crawford was a bear of a man with a big barrel-chest covered in hair and thick with the hard-earned muscle of a man who worked at a manual labor job his entire life.

"Dad," said Scott calmly, "I need you to listen to me; I'm begging you to listen to what I have to say. I didn't do this without thinking it through."

"Listen to you! I busted my ass so you could go to college. Woke up at four a.m. to haul you to swim practices, paid for elite swim leagues so you could get a partial scholarship, and now you're gonna throw it away? No! No, Scott. Just no!"

"Matt, let him speak," said Lorraine softly, her small hand resting on his thick forearm. Matt looked at his wife and felt the tug of his heart as always. She was the most beautiful woman in the world. He would do anything for her, but in this, he wasn't giving in. Twenty years of working construction jobs, pouring concrete, lifting beams. His hands are calloused and aching from years of building other people's homes while he rented a shithole for his own family.

"Lorraine, I love you, honey, but this boy is going back to college. I will not let him quit this!"

"Dad, I left because I've joined the Coast Guard." His father started to speak, but Scott stood to his own full height of six-foot-five and stared into his father's eyes. "Dad, after 9-11, all of my friends seemed to go off and join the military. I had the scholarship, and, well, I didn't want to disappoint you and Mom, but my heart just isn't in it. Now, I've done my research, and I've gone to all the recruiters. I'm a big man like my pops."

His father couldn't help but let a grin slip at the statement. He was big like his pops, but his muscles weren't won from manual labor, rather from time spent in the gym and the pool, the muscles of a young man with his entire life ahead of him.

"The Army or Marines would be happy to have me, but honestly, that's too far from the water for me. I'd love to go into the Navy, but I can't be assured I'd be assigned to a ship. The Coast Guard is my choice. They're doing amazing work in assisting with homeland security. The boarding of ships off our own coasts is critical, Pop. I know I can make a difference, and I can finish my degree as I go."

His father chewed on his lower lip and looked toward his wife, a sweet smile on her own lips, the slight tilt of her head sending him the message that their son was becoming a man, choosing his own path.

Matt knew he was going to lose this argument. It wasn't like his son was a child. He was a twenty-year-old man, full grown in every way.

"You promise me you'll finish your degree?" he asked quietly.

"I promise, Pop, you have my word." He stared at his father, seeing the pride mixed with pain in his eyes. He knew the sacrifices his parents made for him, but it was time to do his part, and somehow, he knew the Coast Guard was the right choice for him.

"I've always been proud of you, Scott. You've never done one thing to disappoint me or make your mother and I ashamed to be your parents. I just... I just always wanted better for you."

"Pops," said Scott, reaching out to grip his father's shoulder. "Pops, you've given me the best of everything. The best birthdays, Christmases, the most loving home a kid could ask for. I need to do this, Pops. I need to serve my country." His father nodded, tears shining in his big brown eyes.

"You'll come home and see us?" he asked.

"You know I will, Pops. I go to basic training on the first of the month. I'll be gone for a while, but I'll come back here before my first assignment begins. It should be a piece of cake for me, Pops. I mean, a circuit swim, tread water for 5 minutes, and jump off a six-foot platform and swim a hundred meters? Easy." He grinned.

"And the physical out of the water portion?" asked his father with a hint of doubt.

"Twenty-nine push-ups in sixty seconds, thirty-eight sit-ups in sixty seconds, run a mile and a half in under twelve minutes and fifty-one seconds, and sit-and-reach sixteen point five inches. I can do this, Pops."

"Ship is an awful small place for big men like us," his dad said thoughtfully. Scott stepped closer to his father and pulled him in for a big grizzly hug.

"I got this, Pops." Matt nodded at his son, slapping his back with a big thump of his hammer-sized fist.

"If you don't write to your mother, I'll ride out to that ship and drag your ass back home," he grinned. Scott laughed, nodding at his parents.

"I love you both, you know. You've given me everything. Now let me do something to give back."

It was four months later when Scott returned home, somehow bigger, stronger, and more agile than before. His strong bearing was more evident, his maturity shining through the stark white of his uniform. Three days later, he shipped out on a four-hundred-and-eighteen-foot Legend-class Cutter.

With one hundred and twenty-two crew members, he soon discovered he was the largest man on the

ship.

His Pops was right. Ships are not a place to forget your height. In the first month, he slammed

his head more times than he could count and bruised his shins to the point of bleeding. But he learned.

And he loved it.

After a year of service, he was discovering that he was in exactly the place he should be, never

regretting his choice. His skills as a rescue swimmer and as the most intimidating man on the ship

helped with more than a few ship boardings, stopping drug traffickers, sinking boat rescues, and refugee

boat searches and rescues.

The Coast Guard's skills were sought after by the Navy to help train their own sailors in the

proper and safe way to board ships, just as the first gulf war developed. He felt fulfilled. In his

downtime, he would take a class or do what he'd always done to relax, draw. Sometimes it was

something he saw while sailing. Other times, it was random drawings but always envisioning the

drawing on something he would own one day.

By the end of his first tour, he knew he would re-enlist. He used his signing bonus to purchase

his first Harley-Davidson and put his artistic abilities to the test. He designed and painted the tank

himself, the elaborate scene of a ship in high seas, fighting Neptune and the elements. The vivid blues

and whites almost leaped off the metal. It didn't matter where he was; he would get stopped and asked

about the design.

Twelve years later, while trying to decide if he would re-enlist once again, he was approached

on the street of a small town in Virginia by a beast of a man. Scott sat at the outdoor coffee shop and watched as the man admired the work on his tank, inwardly grinning. Standing, he approached the stranger with the full thick salt-and-pepper beard.

"Can I help you?" he asked softly. The man turned quickly, his eyes looking upward, something he rarely had to do. He noticed the deep scar on the other man's face and nodded. It wasn't uncommon. Skull often felt as though it was the first thing people saw, and to be fair, it was big and ugly. He could thank an Asian drug runner for that souvenir. Although he did get his own licks in before killing the bastard.

"This yours?" he asked. Scott nodded. "Just admiring the work on the tank. Who did it?"

"Me."

"You?" he questioned. "Fucking grade-A work, brother. I'm Eric Stanton, but my team calls me Ghost." He extended a big rough hand to the other man and watched it disappear into the bear's grip.

"Scott Crawford, but they call me Skull."

"Skull?"

"Yea. I'm a Chief in the Coast Guard. Cracked my skull more than a few times on the ships yet never once bled," he grinned.

"Ah, well," laughed the other man, "done that a few times myself. Retired Navy SEAL, brother. Nice to meet you. You still in?"

"Sort of. I mean, yes. I'm at the end of my enlistment and trying to decide if I want to continue." Ghost nodded and grinned, the wheels spinning out of control in his head.

"Feel like another cup of coffee?" Ghost asked him. Scott looked at the man, and something inside him said this was another one of those moments when he was in the right place, the place he was supposed to be.

"Yea, brother, sure."

Two hours later, he'd learned of the Steel Patriots MC and the work they were doing in their little corner of Virginia. He also learned that they were starting a garage to build custom bikes and cars and needed someone who could do custom artwork and paint jobs, as well as the mechanical. Scott was intrigued.

"So, living quarters are provided?"

"Yep," smiled Ghost. "Why don't you follow me up there and see what we have?" Scott agreed, following the big man up the mountain road and meeting the rest of the team. Forty-eight hours later, he was turning in his paperwork for retirement.

He never looked back.

CHAPTER TWO

"Yea, Pops, that was our bike on the cover," he smiled into the phone. "I know. It's crazy, right?"

"I'm so proud of you, Scott," his father said in a shaky voice. Skull knew his father was fighting back his emotions and felt the familiar feeling of joy that his father was indeed proud of him. "You made all the right decisions, and you fulfilled your promise to your mother and me. We have a son who is a college graduate, a part-owner of a business, and creating some of the most amazing motorcycles on the planet."

"Thanks, Pops. Listen, I gotta run, but I'll see you and Mom soon, okay?"

"We love you, Scott."

"Love you too, Pops."

Skull pulled his boots on and headed toward the garage, darting into the kitchen first to grab a breakfast sandwich. The morning chaos was almost too much for him.

In the span of just a few weeks, four new lives screamed their little lungs out at the compound. First was a healthy baby girl born to Doc and Bree. Eva Irene weighed in at eight pounds and one ounce, her flaming red curls giving no doubt as to who her mother was.

Forty-eight hours later, Whiskey and Kat gave birth to another girl, Juliette Rose, seven pounds even. Her white-blonde hair was so much like her mother's, her hazel eyes like her father's.

Four days later, Taylor and Tango gave birth to a boy, Chase Maxwell. Six pounds, six ounces of pure little boy.

And finally, just one week later, Ghost and Grace gave birth to a second son, Eric Ryan. Grace insisted on having her tubes tied while she was there, and Gabi gladly obliged. Eight children, seven under the age of eighteen months, now graced their compound. Three more were on the way in the summer, all at the same time.

Tinley, expecting triplets, walked every day, ensuring that she got her exercise in. She was doing extremely well with her weight and blood pressure, everyone very happy with how she was handling the pregnancy, but damn, that woman made Skull nervous every time he looked at her protruding belly.

Now working as the Steel Patriots new accountant, Tinley propped her feet on a stool in the garage and began reviewing the invoices as she always did at the end of the month. As the bell above the door rang, she stood to see a tiny little woman enter.

"Hello, welcome to Steel Garage. Can I help you?" she said in a perky, breathless voice. Just standing quickly exhausted her with the addition of the trio heavy on her body.

"I hope so," she said, smiling at the other woman. Tinley couldn't help but think she looked like a tiny fairy doll. She couldn't be more than five-feet-two, her tight body reminding her of a gymnast. She had blonde hair curling down her back and the biggest green eyes she'd ever seen. "I'm looking for someone named Skull."

"Oh yes, Skull, Scott is his real name. Let me get him for you." She opened the door to the garage and called for Skull, who looked up and smiled at Tinley, walking toward her as he began wiping his hands on the paint-stained rag.

"What's up? You need anything?" he asked, his voice laced with concern for his friend's wife.

"No, there's a woman here to see you."

"A woman? For me?" he said incredulously.

"Yes," she laughed, "is that so unusual?"

"Well, yea, but I'll come in. Give me a minute to wash my hands." Tinley nodded and walked back into the office.

"He'll be right with you. I'm Tinley, by the way. My husband works here as well."

"Willa," she said, smiling. "How much longer for you?"

"Oh, well, longer than you think. I'm having triplets."

"Oh my God!" she gasped. "Really?"

"Really, my husband is a twin. He and his brother both live and work here, and, well, it sounds strange, but my daughter from a first relationship is married to his brother."

"Wow, interesting at Christmas, right?" The woman smiled up at her, her eyes alight with curiosity and humor.

"No doubt," laughed Tinley. "Oh, here he is. Scott? This is Willa... Willa... Scott."

You could have knocked all two hundred and fifty pounds of him over with a feather. Skull stared at the little pixie, his heart beating so hard against his chest, he was certain she could hear it. Her smile was so wide and bright, he could feel himself hardening in his coveralls.

"Scott?" yelled Tinley.

"Oh, sorry," he said, reaching out a hand. Her tiny hand was lost inside his. "Scott Crawford, but they call me Skull. We've been communicating back and forth on e-mail and text."

"Yes, sorry about not calling ahead of time. I just moved here a few weeks ago to be closer to my brothers. I was hoping maybe you could show me the design so far."

She looked uncertain and fearful. Skull worried that his size was intimidating her, so he stepped back a few inches. Nodding, he opened the door for her. As she stepped through, all eyes turned to her and then back to Skull, who shook his head slightly.

Pulling back the tarp, he revealed the sleek motorcycle, chrome gleaming in the light of the garage. The tank wasn't finished yet, but the outline of the design of the Army logo surrounded by all the medals and ribbons her brother received was exactly what she'd pictured.

"It's beautiful," she said with tears in her eyes. "Your work is beautiful, just perfect."

"Thank you," he beamed. She continued to cry and then brought her hands to cover her face, sobbing as she did. Skull wasn't very experienced with women, but when one was crying this much, he was pretty sure it wasn't normal.

"Hey, hey, it's okay. If you don't like something, we can change it," he said, looking at the bike and then at the shocked faces of his brothers. She shook her head, and he reached out, his big paw lightly resting on her shoulder. Willa turned into the heat of his body, burying her face in his lower chest, her head barely hitting his rib cage.

"Whoa, hey, sweetheart, it's okay. What's wrong?" he said, holding her still. By this time, Blade, Whiskey, and Razor noticing that she was crying and not out of happiness, stood from their work and gathered around Skull and the little woman creating puddles on their garage floor.

"I don't know what to do," she hiccupped, her shoulders jerking violently. "My b-brothers… they're m-missing… both of them."

"Okay, okay, one is active duty, right?" he asked. She nodded. "The other retired?" She nodded again. "When did you see them last?"

"M-my first night in town. I rented an apartment in the valley, and they drove out to help me unpack. I could tell something was wrong. They both seemed nervous or something and kept looking out the window. When I asked them what was wrong, they wouldn't answer me. They left, and I haven't been able to get a hold of them since. My younger brother's unit commander said he's AWOL."

"Okay, sweet girl, it's okay," said Skull, gently rubbing her back. "Let's get you home, and we'll figure this out." A fresh flood of tears started, and he nearly cracked in two at the sound. Shaking her head, she looked up at him, those green eyes begging him for help.

"I... I can't. Someone broke into my apartment last night, trashed everything. I stayed at a bed and breakfast last night. I... I don't know what to do. I have no one. I have nowhere to go."

"Sure, you do, honey," he said resolutely, sucking in a deep breath. "You have me."

"You?" she asked suspiciously. "I don't even know you. I mean, I barely know anything about you. I can't ask you for help. I mean, why would you help?" Skull stared down at the woman and, for a minute, wanted to give a smart-ass retort. Damn woman should know better than to cry on his chest and think he wouldn't help, but he held back and took a deep breath.

"You know enough about me. I'm retired Coast Guard. I work full-time at Steel Garage. My brothers are all retired military, and the Steel Patriots MC helps people who need it. It's that simple."

Willa stepped back and looked at the circle of men now staring at her. Wiping her eyes, she shook her head.

"I don't understand any of this," she said, staring from one man to the next.

"It's simple," said Razor, "we help the underdog, and we always help a lost brother. We may not have served with your brothers, but they're still our brothers. Get it?" She shook her head, and Razor let a small grin slip.

"I'm sorry. I'm a software geek, not a soldier or sailor, or what do you call Marines?"

"Marines," smiled Whiskey.

"Oh, right. Sorry. I just don't understand what's happening. I can't go home, or at least, I don't want to go home; I can't get a hold of either of my brothers, and I'm just feeling so lost." Skull stared down at the woman. She was the tiniest person he'd ever been around other than a child. He wondered if her brothers were small men, then decided it didn't matter. He was already formulating excuses in his head as to why he shouldn't be near her.

"Listen, why don't we go up to the restaurant and talk with Ghost? He's our team lead and head of the Steel Patriots. Let's get some basic information from you. Once we have that, I'll go with you back to your place and see if we can find something. We'll gather your clothes, and you can stay here." She started to protest, and Tinley stepped in, smiling at the other woman.

"We have a guest cottage, Willa. It's lovely, and it's safe and secure on our property. We'd love to have you as our guest." She smiled at the other woman, noticing her uncertainty. Finally, nodding, she followed Whiskey and Skull out the back-bay doors.

"This place is huge," she said, looking around the property. Whiskey waited for Skull to take the lead on the conversation, but when he said nothing, simply staring ahead at the restaurant, he spoke up.

"It is," he grinned. "We own the garage, the restaurant, a clinic, a gym, and now there's a salon on-site as well. We own several hundred acres, and most of us have homes on the property. Those that don't live in the barn. It's sort of an apartment complex if you will."

She nodded, looking around the landscape, taking everything in. Staring at the back of the man she now knew was Scott, she sucked in a deep breath. He was enormous, and if she were being honest, he frightened her a bit. Not just by his size, but the big scar stretching across his face made him appear more intimidating somehow.

Willa adjusted her eyes to the dimly lit restaurant, glancing down for just a fraction of a second, just long enough to slam into the back of Scott. He seemed to barely notice, but she bounced back like a bad penny nearly falling on her ass.

"Sorry," she whispered. He turned and stared down at her, confused at first, then nodded.

"Have a seat over there, Willa," said Whiskey. "I'll go get Ghost." He tugged on the arm of Skull, pulling him a few feet away from the table, his eyes boring holes into him.

"What?"

"What? What the fuck is wrong with you?" he asked.

"What do you mean? I'm trying to help that woman." Skull looked back at the blotchy, red face of Willa Ross and then back to the face of frustration on his teammate.

"Are you? You've barely spoken to her and didn't even notice when she slammed into you." Whiskey folded his arms across his big chest, staring into the face of his brother. He knew that Skull was self-conscious about the scar. He also knew that he wasn't very good with women, at least not talking to them.

"She doesn't weigh as much as my hammer, dude. How could I notice that bumping into me."

"Just... just be nice. Try talking to her, and I'll find Ghost." Whiskey walked away, shaking his head at his friend. He knew why Skull was self-conscious of the scar on his face, but honestly, the brother was a great catch for some woman. Maybe not this one but someone. He was honest, smart, creative, and a fucking hard worker. *Damn. Now I sound like the women.*

Skull turned to see the tiny woman seated at the table. For the first time, he really looked at her. She was dressed in a pair of dark jeans, a v-neck t-shirt hugging her barely-there curves, and a pair sandals with a tiny blocked heel. She wore very little makeup but, in his opinion, didn't need it. He pulled out the chair on the other side of the table and sat down, smiling uncomfortably at her.

"I'm sorry I brought this to your doorstep," she said quietly.

"Don't be sorry. It's what we do for a living." She nodded. "You-you said you develop software, right?"

"Yes. I mean, I did. I mean, I do," she laughed, shaking her head. "I own my own company, but I sold my biggest creation a few years ago. I developed a software program for cellular providers."

"Really? What does it do?" he asked, intrigued.

"It allows the provider to have visibility into potential homeland security threats by the user." Skull's eyebrows raised, and he stared at Willa. "It's not ghosting or anything. It's simply hitting on buzz words that will send a notification to homeland for further investigation. The buzz words must connect in some way. I mean, I can't text you and say, 'let's blow this place,' and it be flagged. It would have to be a series of comments or words, like 'let's blow this place,' 'don't forget the fertilizer,' 'remember the detonators,' although I suppose that's painfully obvious," she said, biting her lip.

"No, no, I get it. That's great. I thought there was already something like that in place."

"Yes, it's mine," she smiled again. "I developed this more than ten years ago. Back then, no one wanted to give me the time of day. Then WikiLeaks happened, suspicion of election fraud, threats against U.S. embassies and bases, and every other crazy thing on the planet. Suddenly, everyone was knocking at my door. I sold it three years ago. I'm working on several things right now, but it's all stuff I can do from my home. Which is why I moved out here to be closer to my brothers."

Skull nodded, then stood seeing Whiskey, Ghost, and Zulu walking toward them. Following closely behind was Ace.

"Willa, this is our team lead, Ghost. You met Whiskey earlier. That's Zulu, and over there is Ace. Boys, this is Willa Ross. We're building the bike for her brother, who is retiring from the Army, but when she got here today, she informed us that her home was broken into yesterday, and her brothers are now missing. One is considered AWOL." Skull felt a shove at his shoulder as Whiskey pushed him around the table to take the seat closer to Willa. He wanted to deck his brother but instead simply growled and moved chairs.

"I'm sorry for your troubles, Miss Ross," said Ghost.

"Willa, please, it's just Willa. I didn't mean to drop my problems in your lap. I really was just driving around trying to stay away from my apartment when I thought I would come and look at the bike. Honestly? When I was surrounded by all those big men in the garage, I suddenly couldn't hold it in any longer. It was like an instant feeling of protection that I've been missing these last few weeks."

"Are you afraid?" asked Skull.

"Yes. Not of you," she said quickly. "Yes, I'm afraid. If you haven't noticed, I'm a little on the small side, and I'm smart enough to recognize my limitations."

"I noticed," mumbled Skull. Willa's face flushed a delightful shade of pink, and Whiskey grinned at his friend.

"Yes, well, being small in this world isn't all it's cracked up to be."

"Willa, start at the beginning," said Ghost. "Tell us everything." She nodded.

"Okay. Well, I've been in contact with Scott for several months about my brother's motorcycle. We've never met, but we communicated via e-mail and text messaging. As I told him, our parents died when I was eleven. Craig, my brother you're building the bike for, was just twenty at the time. He was already in the Army but fought to be allowed to have custody of my brother and me. Kevin was just eight years old."

"Damn," muttered Zulu, "that's tough. How did the Army react?"

"They were really great. My brother was able to prove he was a fit parent, and they assigned him permanently to Fort Bragg. When I turned eighteen, he was able to deploy, and I took over caring for Kevin. We're all adopted, so we make a very interesting family. Craig's parents were African American, and Kevin's were from the Philippines. We make a great United Nations Christmas card," she smiled. The others grinned at the woman, nodding.

"Craig gave up everything to provide for us. He rarely dated, saved every penny he made to help us have the life we wanted and needed. Kevin and I always had part-time jobs and helped as well. There was no drama, no fighting, no drugs, no alcohol, just normal sibling behavior. We were normal, other than not having parents. When Craig decided to finally retire, I thought this was my chance to do something great for him. My software sold for millions a few years ago, so I have the resources."

"What happened when you moved here?" asked Whiskey.

"It was three weeks ago. Craig and Kevin both said they would come down and help me get everything unpacked. They were supposed to be here by noon but didn't get to my place until nearly five. They never even said why they were late. I was just so happy to see them both." She shook her head with the memory, nibbling on her lower lip. "Craig, he seemed normal to me at first, but Kevin was nervous. He kept looking out my front window, and Craig would give him a dirty look."

"Kevin? Is he in the Army as well?" asked Ghost.

"Yes. He joined to follow in Craig's footsteps. They left my place about seven or eight, I guess. Over the next few days, I was pretty much obsessed with getting my place in order. I'm a bit of a neat freak, and when it comes to my computers, I'm crazy obsessive. I kept feeling as though someone was watching me when I would leave the apartment. I called Craig, but they said he was on leave, which I knew. He's basically taking the remainder of his leave before retirement. But he didn't answer his cell phone either." All heads nodded at her.

"When I tried to call Kevin on his cell, he didn't answer, so I called the base. His commanding officer said he was AWOL. I couldn't believe it. He would never go AWOL, never! Neither have answered their cell phones or e-mails. Yesterday morning, I left for the grocery store, and when I returned, everything in my apartment was trashed. Computers were broken, furniture destroyed, pictures torn, ev-everything." She wiped the tears settling on her cheeks and shook her head.

"Did you file a police report?" asked Ghost.

"I did. I called them immediately. Nothing is salvageable that I could see, nothing. I called Kevin's CO again and told him what happened. I said I thought that it might be connected somehow to his disappearance, but he wasn't inclined to agree with me. This just doesn't make any sense at all."

"Are you working on anything worth stealing right now?" asked Skull. Her head shot up, and the look was clear—everything I work on is important. "I mean, you know what I mean." Blushing, she nodded.

"Yes, yes, I know what you mean. I'm working on a system to improve medical records keeping and another for tracking museum artworks and sculptures. Nothing earth-shattering or dealing with national security."

"Did your brothers say anything? Did they talk about anything they were working on?" asked Zulu.

"No, nothing, but they rarely spoke about their service time. I understood. Honestly, I didn't ask because I knew what they would say. All I know is that my brothers would have never left without telling me where they were going. We spoke every week without exception for the last ten years. No matter where they were, we always spoke. Something is wrong."

Ghost nodded, giving a silent look to the men at the table. Standing, Skull held out his big paw.

"Let's go visit your place and see what we can find," he said, staring down at her. Willa looked at the table of men, feeling hopeful for the first time in weeks. Sliding her small hand into his, she nodded.

"Thank you. Thank you all for helping."

"Don't thank us yet," said Ghost. "My experience tells me that something isn't right here, Willa. You're right about that, but that only means something is very wrong, and very wrong could mean anything." Nodding at the older man, she straightened her back, staring up at him.

"Right."

CHAPTER THREE

"What do you think?" asked Zulu, looking at his three brothers. Ace, previously the quietest member of their team, spoke first. His transformation was directly related to the love of his life, Charlotte, Charlie.

"I think one or both of the brothers were hiding something that she got caught in the middle of. The question is whether they've somehow intentionally or unintentionally involved her and placed her in danger. I'll check them out and see what I can come up with." He turned and walked toward his office, the others grinning as he walked away.

"Man, I love Charlie for what she's done for him," smiled Whiskey. The chuckles of the others echoed his sentiments.

"Whiskey? Give Ivan a call as well. I don't know. Something is really wrong here. I mean, Kevin is stationed at Andrews, and Craig is retiring from Bragg. They're pretty far apart, so why did they drive up together?" Ghost watched through the window as Skull walked with Willa back toward the garage. He could see him already pulling his coveralls off his upper body, the big arms stretching the fabric to its limit.

"Do you think she knew about us?" asked Zulu.

"I don't know," said Ghost, "but it seems unlikely she didn't. I mean, the woman is a computer genius of some sort. I know if it were Ace, he would have known our shoe sizes before coming in here, but then again, she's not Ace, and she's not ex-military."

"Weren't Hawk and Eagle originally out of Bragg?" asked Whiskey. Ghost nodded. "Maybe we send them down to ask questions."

"Not Eagle, Tinley is too close. I know they say she has another six to eight weeks, but damned if I'll believe it looking at her," he smiled.

"How about Hawk and Blade? He's done with that old Chevelle. The owner picked it up this morning. We have a Charger coming in tomorrow, but he could wait a few days to start on it."

"Sounds good, but I think maybe Ace is the better one to send with Blade. Let's get them down there and see what they can find out. I don't want to call Admiral Crossing. Do we have any other contacts we can count on?" asked Ghost.

"General Donan," said Zulu. "He was part of that mission we did in Haiti. Seemed like a stand-up dude to me, and he's been helpful over the years." Ghost nodded, and Zulu walked back toward his own home and office to call the General.

"Shit never gets easier, does it?" asked Ghost to no one in particular, although it was just him and Whiskey left in the room.

"Is it supposed to?" he laughed. "Listen, man, we started this to help the little man or woman, and that damned sure is one of the littlest women I've ever seen. We decided a long time ago we only take the jobs we want to take on. We're still doing that, Ghost, but if it ever gets to be too much, we don't need to do this any longer. We've done our time; we've served our country. This? All of this is just extra."

"Could you stop?" he asked Whiskey. The other man's face was filled with shock and then regret. "If we decided yesterday that we wouldn't do this shit any longer, could you honestly have turned that woman away today?"

"Fuck no," he growled.

"That's my point, brother. We can't seem to say no. It's just that now we all have families. I have two sons, for fuck's sake!" He ran his long fingers through his graying hair.

"So, maybe we recruit some new guys. We've talked about it before, but maybe now it's time to actively recruit. Have some of the guys reach out to people they served with. Let Ace do backgrounds before we do any face-to-face meetings." Ghost tugged on his beard and nodded.

"Do it. Ask everyone to think about it long and hard. They should only reach out to men—or women—they truly trusted and would continue to trust with their own life or ours. That's it."

"Great! Let's grow the family, Dad."

"Fuck you."

CHAPTER FOUR

The silence in the cab of the truck was nearly deafening to Willa. Normally, she would have her radio blasting and singing along with no one in particular as other drivers looked at her as if she'd lost her mind. She gave a sideways glance toward the towering body in the driver's seat and shifted uncomfortably in her seat. Her feet barely touched the floorboards of the huge vehicle.

Scott Crawford, or Skull, was probably the biggest man she'd ever stood next to. It wasn't just his impressive height; it was the bulk of his body as well. Noticing the hint of tattoos peeking out beneath the neck of his t-shirt, she couldn't resist asking.

"Do your tattoos have specific meaning?" she asked, smiling at him.

"Some." She waited patiently for him to continue, his silence blanketing the truck once more. Not able to control her own urges, she spoke again.

"Some? Which ones?" she asked again, eyeing him with curiosity.

"A few on my chest."

"I see," she said, looking out the window. He seemed perturbed that she was in his truck, somehow an intolerable reality. "Have I made you angry in some way?"

"What?" The look of shock on his face nearly made her laugh. He was obviously not used to causal conversations with women or being teased by them.

"I'm teasing, sort of. I'm just trying to get to know you, Scott, and it seems every time I try to have a conversation, you reply with one-word responses or act as though I'm putting you out in some way. I'm sorry that all this has happened, and I brought it to you, but you did offer to help."

"Why? I mean, why do you want to get to know me?"

"Why?" she asked, staring at him with disbelief.

"Yea, I mean, why would someone like you want to know someone like me."

"Someone like me? Someone like you? I'm confused here. You're human, a male human. I'm a human, a female human. Typically, those species like to get to know one another. What am I missing here?"

"You're... you're beautiful and successful and smart. You look like the tiny ballerina that dances inside little girls' jewelry boxes. I mean, my hand would completely cover your head. I'm a bull in a china shop on a good day. I build motorcycles and cars. I paint them. I get greasy and dirty, and most of the time, I live with an eternal cloud of motor oil cologne hanging over my head. I have more scars than the obvious one on my face. I have trouble finding clothes that fit, which means my wardrobe is pathetic. We're just different, and whether you know me or not, we're still going to help you."

Willa could not believe the words this man was saying. She'd never met a man as insecure about their physical appearance as she was, yet in a totally different way. It was obvious the scar was at the core of his insecurity, but big boy had other issues as well.

"Scott, Skull, what should I call you?"

"Either is fine."

"Scott, I'm a tiny person. You're right. I can't do a thing about that. You're... not tiny. You can't do a thing about that. We are *both* smart, successful people. You've served our nation, protected people like me, and I find that more than just an admirable quality. I appreciate that you think I'm beautiful, but that doesn't mean anything. I owe that to whoever my biological parents were. You're handsome. You owe that to your parents."

"No woman has ever described me as handsome, Willa." He ran a big finger down the crease of the scar, wincing as if it was still painful.

"The scar?" Skull nodded. "How did it happen?"

"We stopped a boat we suspected of carrying drugs. We were right. One of the men on board turned out to be head of the crime family. I was the biggest guy on the ship, and I suppose he saw that as an invitation to prove how good he was. He just wasn't as good as me."

"Well, I'm glad about that. Thank you for risking your life for your country, although I sincerely hope you don't have to do that again. Look, I'm just trying to get to know you. I get that you have a hard time finding clothes. Guess what? So do I, so I understand that clothes *do not* always make the man or woman. Half the time, I'm shopping in the teen sections, which is humiliating when you're trying to look professional. If we're touting insecurities, I have no womanly curves, Scott, none. I get lost in crowds. I can't find shoes to fit, and I'm such a geek that half the time, I don't even notice there are people around me if I'm on my computer."

"You may not understand this, Scott, but I like the way you look. I mean, I barely know you at all, but I like how big you are. A woman my size wants to feel like she's protected. I'm just saying it's attractive to me."

"You… you don't have a boyfriend?" he asked, feeling the heat rise in his cheeks.

"I did. We broke up more than three years ago. We dated for almost four years, and in all that time, I never felt safe when we were out. I never once felt as though if someone tried to attack us that he could or would protect me. Craig and Kevin hated him," she laughed.

"Why?"

"A lot of reasons, but mostly because he wasn't the guy to open doors or walk on the street side of the sidewalk, or…" She looked out the window at the passing trees, the pain of her missing brothers filling her gut.

"Why else? Why didn't they like him?" he asked with a hint of anger lacing his deep voice.

"He didn't hit me, if that's what you're wondering. He knew enough to not touch me, but he wasn't exactly kind with his words. One birthday he tried to give me breast augmentation as my gift."

"He tried to give you a boob job?" Skull winced, realizing that his statement came out way too loud and way too angry, but Willa just laughed.

"Yes. He had a friend who was a surgeon, and he got a deal. That's what every girl wants, a deal on new boobs." She couldn't help but laugh at that, and soon Scott was laughing as well.

"What else?" he chuckled.

"I don't know. He just wasn't very kind to me sometimes. He rarely had a full-time job, which really angered my brothers. When I sold my software, I think he thought I would be his meal ticket. He wanted me to fund his start-up, but I refused."

"He left you?" asked Skull with a serious look.

"He did. I wasn't even upset, so that tells you how I felt. My brothers were thrilled. Anyway, the biggest reason they hated him was one time when we were all walking around downtown Chicago, there was this big protest, and I was really feeling scared. I mean, there were a lot of people, and there was pushing and shoving, people were angry. My brothers kept pulling me closer to them because Alan was pretty much ignoring me. When my brother asked him what he was going to do if we were attacked, Alan said, 'I'm not worried about it. I only have to outrun the slowest person,' and he pointed to me. Kevin wanted to kill him. Craig clocked him in the jaw."

"Good for him. I would have killed him," he said through his clenched jaw.

"Yea, well, it was a wake-up call for me. He wasn't the man who would ever protect me. I don't need someone to take care of me or provide for me. I can do that. I can help with that as a couple. I'm smart enough to know that at my size, though, I need help physically. I mean, I can't even reach things on the top shelf at the grocery store."

"At least you know that. We see a lot of women who recognize that too late. Zulu and Gunner run our gym. You should get with them. They might be able to teach you some things that would help."

"Really? That would be amazing," she said excitedly. He gave her a quick smile and turned his attention back to the GPS directions leading him to her apartment.

Pulling up in front of the historic building, Skull stepped around the truck and helped her down. His huge hands wrapped around her tiny waist and easily lifted her to the sidewalk.

"Thank you," she said, blushing. Boldly reaching upward, she ran her fingers over the deep scar, wincing at the thought of how painful it must have been. "It's not so bad, you know. It makes you look dangerous and sexy at the same time, and your beard almost completely covers it."

"Sexy?" he grinned. "So, you think I'm sexy?"

"I didn't say that," she huffed, blushing. "I said the scar makes you look... I mean, some people might think it makes you look that way." He gave her a serious look and nodded. She was cute when she was ruffled. The problem was, she was fucking beautiful the rest of the time.

"Lead the way," he said, waving his big hand toward the door. Willa walked toward the door to the side of the old general store, now a museum.

"There are only four apartments in the building, but I took this one because it has views of the mountains on one side and the valley on the other. I'm not sure if I want to buy or not, so I'm on a six-month lease until I decide, although I may seriously consider moving after this." As they took the steps to the second floor, Skull stepped in front of her. Reaching the landing, he looked down the narrow hallway and saw only one door.

"Is there only one apartment on this floor?" he asked.

"Yes. Each floor has one apartment, which is the other reason I took it. They're big for apartments. This one was completely renovated with an open concept loft feel, very SoHo Tribeca feel to it." Skull looked at her, confused. "You know, New York city? The trendy neighborhoods of SoHo and Tribeca?"

"Sorry, I don't like big cities," he said, walking toward the door. He noticed the crime scene tape and carefully ran his fingers around the door, feeling for any trips or triggers. As he touched the door, it easily swung open.

"They broke my locks and the doorknob. I can't shut it at all." Skull ducked beneath the tape and pushed the door open further, taking a step inside the space. He could imagine how beautiful it once was, but right now, it was a disaster. He turned, hearing a sniff, to see Willa with tears in her eyes.

"I'm sorry. It's just such a mess and, as you can see, nearly everything will need to be replaced. Even if it could be repaired, I don't think I want to touch it ever again."

"Don't be sorry, Willa," he said, squeezing her hand. "It is a mess, but it's not your fault. Did they touch your clothes?" She shook her head. "Okay, go get what you think you'll need. If there are things you can preserve, take them as well." She nodded and moved toward the bedroom as Skull opened his phone, taking a video of the space to send to Ace and Ghost.

She was right. The entire apartment had been trashed. What he couldn't figure out was why no one heard the noise unless the other apartment dwellers had been at work. Dishes were broken on the concrete floors, furniture overturned and broken, paintings ripped with a knife; everything was destroyed. Someone was looking for something. They weren't just sending her a message.

Walking around the big 'U' shape, he followed the floor plan through the kitchen and dining area down a hallway to the two bedrooms. That's where he found Willa on the cold concrete floor, her knees pulled to her chest, sobbing softly. Skull stood for a moment, unsure of what to do. Finally putting his phone away, he sat down next to her and pulled her into his embrace.

"It's okay, Willa. It's okay, honey. Let it out." She buried her face in his chest, and he gently rubbed his big hands over her back. Skull felt every lean muscle and delicate bone in her body, her slender shape dwarfed by his own troll-like body.

"How did they do all of this in the two hours I was gone?" she asked through hiccups and tears.

"I don't know, honey, but we'll find out. Were you able to gather some clothes?" he asked. Willa nodded and stood as he lifted his big body with her.

"Thank you, Scott, for being here and for helping me." She hugged his waist, pressing her face against his big lower chest. Never in her life had she felt so safe and secure. More than that, she was attracted to this man in a big way, and that shocked her.

"You're welcome, Willa," he grinned. "How about we get some lunch before we head back?"

"I'd like that," she said, smiling up at him. Skull desperately wanted to wipe away her tears, but something else was building within him as well. He wanted to kiss this woman. And not just a peck on the cheek or a 'thank you and goodnight' kiss, no, he wanted to possess this woman, and that was something completely foreign to him.

"Are you okay?" asked Willa, staring at him. He had a far-off, almost territorial animal look on his face.

"Yea, peachy. Let's eat."

CHAPTER FIVE

"Have you found out anything on Craig and Kevin Ross?" asked Ghost, stepping inside Ace's office.

"Some. Some of it we already knew. Craig Ross, forty-two years old, is retiring with twenty-four years of service in the Army, mostly out of Bragg. According to his file, he's five-feet-eleven, a hundred and eighty-five pounds, give or take. He works with deployment helping soldiers prepare to go overseas. He's never had a disciplinary infraction, never been busted down in rank." Ghost nodded, Whisky and Zulu beside him.

"And the brother?" asked Zulu.

"Ah, yes. Well, Kevin Ross is twenty-nine years old. He's been in the Army for almost eleven years now, stationed in a lot of different places but most recently at Bragg with his brother after he was moved from Andrews. Two months ago, he was arrested by the MPs for starting a bar fight."

"Over a girl?" asked Whiskey. All eyes looked at him, and he shrugged. "Hey, it's usually about a girl. Don't give me that look."

"No, it wasn't about a girl, and it wasn't with just anyone. He was throwing punches at his brother, Craig."

"What... the... fuck?" said Ghost in a low growl.

"MPs said when they arrived, two other men were restraining him, and Craig was just sitting with his arms folded, watching his brother lash out. He was screaming obscenities at his brother, calling him every name in the book."

"We need to talk to that bartender and whoever was there that night," said Zulu.

"Blade and I are headed that way," said Ace. "We're going to drive down today and, hopefully, be back in a couple of days. I called General Donan, and he's given us full clearance to investigate, although he was quick to point out we'd mostly likely find Kevin at fault."

"Did he know the Ross brothers?" asked Whiskey.

"He didn't know Kevin well, but he knew Craig. Said he was one of the finest soldiers he'd ever served with. Clean as a whistle, never in any trouble, and completely devoted to his siblings. He thinks the younger brother was into something, and Craig found out." Ghost nodded.

"Okay, you and Blade go down there, but be careful, Ace. If you need any backup, you call us, and we can get there fast."

"Got it," he said, grinning.

"What are you grinning at?" asked Zulu.

"Oh, nothing. It's just that a year ago, it would have been miserable for me to leave here, to leave my sanctuary. Today, not so much, and I have my beautiful wife to thank for that." The three men smiled at their teammate and nodded. It was true. Ace was a completely different person since marrying Charlie. Her influence on them all was evident by their very happy and very healthy sex lives. Charlie wasn't just an amazing wife to Ace. She wrote erotic romance novels that all of the women were in love with, and truth be told, the men had read more than a few as well.

"Just be careful," smiled Ghost. "Let Blade dig into Kevin; you meet with General Donan and figure out what you can about Craig." Ace nodded, grabbing his laptop case and duffel. Following him into the restaurant, Blade walked through the front door with his own duffel slung over his shoulders.

"You ready?" he asked Ace. Ace nodded at the other man. Many of the men on the team were big silent types, but Blade was sort of in a league by himself. At six-foot-one, he wasn't the tallest, nor was he the biggest man, but he was deadly with a knife, hence his name. Although he'd worked primarily in Special Forces, he also worked solo on several missions that, even retired, he refused to talk about.

"Let's go, man," he growled. "I'd like to be at Bragg by dark."

"You afraid of the dark or something?" asked Ace, grinning at his teammate.

"Nope, but that's when I do my best work."

CHAPTER SIX

"How is your salad?" asked Skull with indifference. He wasn't sure a salad could be anything except disgusting, but he was trying to be polite and a little more talkative. It was obvious that Willa needed the conversation, and he was certainly going to do everything he could to make her comfortable.

"It's good," she grinned, "although I doubt if it really matters to you whether or not my salad is any good."

"It matters. If it's bad, we'll send it back."

"That's not what I meant," she murmured, taking another bite. Skull stared at the woman seated across from him. He knew it wasn't what she meant, but he also wasn't sure how to respond to her. Casual conversation wasn't in his wheelhouse and particularly casual conversation with a beautiful woman.

"I'm sorry, Willa. I'm not very good at this." She looked up from her plate, waiting for him to expand. He was squirming in his seat, and she knew that she was making him uncomfortable and, quite honestly, didn't care. "Listen, I work with men all day, every day. I know their wives, but to me, they are all extensions of the guys, and so I tend to speak to them in the same way I speak to the guys."

"Okay, so speak to me that way," she said, smiling.

"Ahhh, I'm not sure that's a good idea," he grimaced.

"Scott, my brothers are both in the military. I think I understand military speak. I've heard more cussing in my lifetime than most men my age, and I definitely don't get offended by the language." He nodded, but she could tell that he wasn't convinced. "Listen, if it's that you don't want to get to know me other than in a professional capacity, that's okay. I understand that I'm not everyone's type."

"Type? Willa, I'm here to help you find your brothers and keep you safe from whoever ransacked your home. I haven't had an official date in almost ten years. I don't have a 'type.'"

"Ten years? Are you telling me you haven't been with a woman in ten years?" she asked with disbelief.

"Uh, no. I'm telling you I haven't had a date in ten years. I've had… encounters with lots of women, safe encounters, but nothing serious, nothing permanent." Skull felt himself turning red, his brain instantly regretting the flatulence flying from his mouth.

"Oh," she blushed. "So, you prefer one-night stands?"

"Geez, Willa! Seriously? No, I don't prefer one-night stands. Sometimes it's just easier to get your itch scratched and walk away. I mean, I haven't been looking for anything permanent, and, believe me, the women who approach me aren't looking for that either."

"I see." Willa's face flushed a crimson shade, her neck blotchy and pink with embarrassment. She was such a fool. Inexperienced with men and unable to distinguish between kindness and flirting, she'd made a mistake with Scott thinking he might be interested in her.

"Willa, Willa, look at me," he prodded, reaching for her hand across the table. "I like you, Willa, really, I do. We hardly know one another, and I need to make sure you're safe and we find your brothers. This doesn't seem ideal to starting a relationship, and let's be honest, honey, I'm probably nothing like you've ever dated before."

"You know, I really wish you'd stop being so self-deprecating and condescending."

"Wait, self what?"

"You're always cutting yourself down! I'm not doing it. You are. I'm trying to get to know you, Scott. You act as though you know better than I do what I want. I'm not a child. I'm a thirty-two-year-old woman who owns her own software development company. I know what and who I like. I know what I like to eat, where I like to live, what clothes I enjoy wearing. Stop treating me like a child!"

Skull swallowed hard, staring at her across the table from him. He'd misinterpreted her questions completely. Yet, he was still having trouble with the realization that she might be interested in him. Still, he couldn't get involved with someone while he was trying to keep her safe and help her find her brothers.

Although let's be honest, he thought, every damn one of his brothers met their women in exactly this scenario.

"I'm sorry if I offended you, Willa." She let out a long slow breath and brushed back the tear sliding down her cheek. It nearly cracked him in two. Reaching across the table, he swiped his big thumb over her tear, bringing the warm, salty drop to his lips.

"I'm just being foolish," she whispered. Willa pushed the plate of greens toward the center of the table, tossing her napkin on top. "I'm finished." Skull nodded at her. Standing, he extended his hand, but she ignored him and turned toward the door of the restaurant. He let out a long sigh, following her as she moved in the direction of the truck.

Seeing the small neighborhood pharmacy across the street, Willa made her way between Skull's truck and the car parked in front of him, darting across the road. Too late, she realized there was a white sedan headed straight for her. In a split second, she froze, bracing for the impact of the vehicle as tires screeched.

Feeling the massive weight hit her body, she rolled in mid-air; the world spun around her as she fell to the pavement, her back braced against something firm and hard. Opening her eyes, she realized it wasn't the car that hit her but Scott, who'd wrapped his arms around her and dove toward the sidewalk, rolling with her enveloped in his embrace. Rolling her to her back, he brushed the blonde hair from her face.

"Are you alright? Willa? Answer me, honey. Are you alright?" She nodded, tears filling her eyes once more. Skull stood, pulling her body against his own as he looked up and down the street.

"I got the license plate," said a lanky teenager, standing behind him. "Saw the guy pull out just as the lady was crossing the street. He never even stopped." Skull nodded, pulling out his phone and sending a text to Ghost and Ace with the license plate number.

"Thanks, kid." The boy nodded and walked back to where his friends were waiting. As Skull turned, he realized Willa was shaking uncontrollably. She was going into shock, and he needed to get her back to the barn. Lifting her into his arms, he wrapped her tightly against the warmth of his body and kissed her temple.

"Come on, baby. Let's get you home."

Damn! What the fuck did you say that for?

CHAPTER SEVEN

"No surprise the plate is a rental," said Ghost, staring at Skull. Willa was upstairs in the on-site treatment room with Gabi and Doc to be checked out. "The car was rented under the name Tom Smith, so I think we can assume it's an alias, but we'll keep checking." Skull nodded, staring back at the door, waiting to hear how Willa was doing.

Ghost looked at his friend and then back at Zulu, Whiskey, and Gunner seated around the table. In all the years they'd known him, Skull had never shown any outward affection toward a woman. He was definitely a man who liked to spend an hour or so alone with a woman, but that was the extent of it. He'd never once been serious about any female—ever.

"You good, Skull?" asked Gunner.

"Hmm? Oh, yea, just worried about Willa. She's so damn small and... small."

"Yea, small," grinned Whiskey. "You mentioned that."

"Yea, small," he said, rubbing his fingers back and forth against the wood grain of the conference table.

"You know, Skull," said Zulu, "I know a thing or two about small women. I mean, you and I aren't that different in size."

"Yea, but Gabi is a lot bigger than Willa. Hell, I've seen kids bigger than her." Whiskey grinned at his friend and then around the table.

"Doesn't mean shit if you like the woman, Skull. You're a good man, and I know that you'd never hurt a woman—ever. I know for a fact that if she's someone you like, you should pursue it."

"No, no, that's not, no, I, damn." Frustrated, he stood, his chair flying backwards and crashing to the floor. "See! That's the kind of shit you can count on from me! Shit flying everywhere. I'm about as graceful as a hippo. I'd crush that poor woman!"

"Brother," said Zulu, "settle down. You would never hurt a woman, never! Skull, if you like the girl, you'll find a way. I've seen what you paint, Skull. Your finesse and elegance with a brush, brother, is unlike anything I've ever seen. Treat Willa with that kind of touch. We all saw the way she was looking at you when you carried her inside. She obviously likes you."

"Me? No, she's just grateful," he groaned.

"Grateful? Brother, she's not a Labrador. She's a woman. She was looking at you in the way women look at men when they want them. We should know, all of us!" said Ghost.

"I don't, hell, I don't have a fucking clue. You guys know that. I haven't dated anyone steady since I was in my early twenties. Like all of you, I didn't have the time or inclination to leave behind a woman and a family. Then this happened," he said, running his fingers over his scar.

"Skull? You don't believe for a minute that women give a shit about that, do you?" asked Whiskey. The other man shrugged his shoulders, looking down at his callused hands, grease stains still beneath a few fingernails. "Brother, listen to me. I think men are way shallower than women. If a dude has a scar, a woman doesn't think twice about it. If a woman has a scar, I think a lot of men look the other way and say no thanks."

"You think so?" he asked, feeling nervous.

"I know so," said Gabi, standing in the door, smiling. She walked toward Zulu and kissed his cheek. "Women don't care about the scar at all. It gives you this air of danger and mystery. It totally fits with the bad-ass biker, ex-military man persona."

"It's not a persona," he growled, giving a quick wink to Gabi.

"I know, I know," said Gabi, smiling. "She likes you, Skull, and she's asking to see you." He moved so quickly toward the door, he nearly knocked over Whiskey and Gunner, his big body brushing against them. Ghost grinned at the room of people.

"Now that is a man bitten."

CHAPTER EIGHT

"Any trouble breathing? Headache? Dizziness?" asked Gabi.

"No, no trouble at all now," said Willa, staring at the beautiful woman hovering above her. Her stunning features nearly knocked her over when she was carried into the room. The silvery-blonde hair fell in waves against her back, her glowing eyes staring directly through her.

"Did you hit the concrete at all?" asked Doc. Shaking her head, she responded.

"No, Scott had me wrapped up before I even knew what was happening. I thought I was hit by the car, but it was him. Is he… did he leave?" Doc grinned at Gabi.

"No, honey, he's downstairs waiting until we say it's okay for him to see you."

"I don't think he likes me," she said quietly.

"What would make you think that?" asked Doc.

"I don't know. He seems to not like all my questions and talking. I mean, I know I can be a bit of a chatterbox sometimes, but I was just trying to get to know him. He seems really sensitive over his size and that scar, but I think he looks incredibly sexy with it." She stopped suddenly, realizing her mistake, and blushed.

"It's okay, Willa. I think he looks sexy with the scar as well, and since I'm married to a man about the same size as him, I think that's sexy too." Gabi winked at the other woman easing her discomfort and smiled.

"I don't know. He didn't seem very receptive to the idea of getting to know me. I mean, I tried everything, and he just kept backing away. He said he hasn't had a long-term relationship in more than ten years, which means he's probably looking for just a one-night stand or something."

"I'm going to go let him know that you're okay. Doc will sit with you until Skull comes back up." Willa nodded as Doc helped her from the exam table.

"He does like you, Willa," said Doc. "My teammates, this motorcycle club, well, we're all a little different. Skull is interesting because he's the only one who served in the Coast Guard. The work he did was every bit as dangerous as those of us who served in Special Forces. Have you seen his artwork?"

"Yes," she nodded, "I mean, I saw the work he did on the tank for my brother. It was amazing." Doc nodded as he sat on the rolling stool across from her, gently touching her knee.

"Yea, he does amazing work on the bikes, but his real talent is in canvas. He paints as a way of coping and reducing stress. My wife and I have three of his paintings in our home, and he did the mural on our daughter's bedroom wall."

"Wow! Really? That's amazing," she said in nearly a whisper.

"He's an amazing man," said Doc. "He's a good man, Willa. He's a man that would be worth the time if you're really interested. But..."

"But?" she asked, turning to stare up at the tall man.

"But, if you're only interested in getting to know him so we can find your brothers, stop now. He deserves better than that, and so do you."

"I-I would never! I mean, I know you don't know me, but I would never do that to him. I want to get to know him. I want to..."

"You want to?" Willa whipped her head around to see the enormous body of Skull standing in the doorway. Doc smiled, clapping a hand on his friend's shoulder.

"She's fine. Nothing broken or bruised, just shaken up." He left the couple standing in the room and headed back downstairs.

"You want to what?" he asked again, taking another step inside the room.

"I-I want to get to know you, really get to know you. I'm sorry if I've been doing it all wrong. I talk too much, and I can be really awkward sometimes," she said, moving closer to him. He shook his head, holding up both hands.

"No, it was my fault. I'm an insecure asshole, and I just couldn't understand why someone so beautiful and talented would want anything to do with me. I admit I thought it was only so we would find your brothers." Willa took another step closer and lifted her hand, placing it against one of his large, raised paws. It was lost in the size of his own.

"I need to find my brothers, but I can find someone else to help if this is awkward. I really do want to get to know you, Scott. Really." He nodded, taking her hand in his own.

"I'm scared I'll hurt you," he said. Her eyes went wide, and he shook his head again. "No, not like hurt your feelings. Like I'm so big, I might physically hurt you." If it were possible, her eyes went wider, and she blushed.

"I'm not sure…"

"Damn! I'm really fucking this up. I'm big. I mean, I'm big all over, but, fuck! I don't want my physical size to hurt you, Willa. I don't want to be the big clumsy bull and step on your foot and crush it, or like today, try to do something to protect you, only to hurt you."

"Scott, you would never hurt me intentionally. I know that. Accidents happen, and we may have lots of accidents as we get to know one another, but I think it's worth a try. Don't you?" Her green orbs stared up at him pleadingly.

"I do, Willa. I absolutely do." He pulled her into his chest, squeezing her gently in a hug. "Do you have everything you need?"

"Yes, my suitcase is still in your truck." Nodding, he pulled her toward the door.

"Let's go back downstairs. Time for us to get to work."

CHAPTER NINE

Ace and Blade walked down the long corridor of the administration building at Fort Bragg. Their stride and bearing let others know they weren't just any visitors; they had been a part of the brotherhood. Approaching the office of General Donan, they slowed to hear low, angered voices coming from behind the door.

"Someone's getting an ass-chewing," said Ace. Blade nodded but listened more intently, picking up on only a few words here and there. Knocking on the door, the voices ceased.

"Come in!" Ace entered first, Blade close behind to see a rather rotund General Donan seated behind his desk. Neither of them had served under him but knew of him and, to be honest, were surprised to see his lack of regard toward his physical state. He was past retirement age but like many, couldn't let go of the only thing he'd ever known. He was thrice divorced, no children, and, apparently, was willing to take any duty station just to remain in the Army he loved.

"General Donan? I'm Alex Mills, but they call me Ace. This is my colleague, Benjamin LeBlanc, but he goes by Blade."

"Yes, Ghost said you boys would be coming down for a visit. Take a seat," he said, pointing to the vacant chairs. "This is Lt. Schumer; he was just leaving." Schumer didn't look like he wanted to leave at all and, in fact, stood stock still for several long seconds before finally turning on his heel and leaving the room.

"We didn't mean to interrupt," said Blade, staring thoughtfully at the general. His wrinkled eyes met Blades suspiciously. "Sorry, we heard arguing outside when we knocked."

"Yes, well, part of the argument is why I believe you're here. We seem to be missing some rather large shipments of weapons, and the person who oversaw that was Kevin Ross." Ace eyed Blade and then turned back to the general.

"You think Kevin Ross was stealing the shipments?"

"No, but I think he was helping whoever did. I think that's what he and his brother were arguing about in the bar that night. Craig Ross is one of the finest soldiers to ever step foot on this base, and his brother could not be more opposite. He's been busted down in rank twice. He's been drunk and disorderly, caught sleeping on duty, you name it and the little shit's been written up for it."

"What's his job?"

"Unit supply specialist," sneered the general as if that weren't an important job. "I tried to get Craig to stay on another five to ten years. We need good men like him. But I understand he gave up a lot when his parents died." The two men nodded, waiting for the general to continue.

"About a year ago, we noticed a shortage on some of our mortar rounds. Mostly 60mm but some 81mm. Not something you can shove in your pocket and walk off with."

"How much of a shortage?" asked Blade.

"Enough to make us suspicious. We investigated, filed the reports, but couldn't find a trail anywhere. Two months later, we lost a shipment, a whole fucking shipment of rocket launchers. How the fuck do you lose a whole shipment? Then six months ago, it was a shipment of M4s."

"And what about all of that made you suspicious of Kevin Ross?" asked Ace.

"He's a fuck up. All three shipments were during his duty. When he was questioned about it, he always had an excuse or alibi."

"But aren't there other men on duty at the same time?" asked Blade.

"Well, yes, of course. Usually, there are at least six men receiving shipments, sometimes more if it's larger, but he was the common denominator in every case."

"And where was his brother?"

"Craig? Why? He has nothing to do with this," said the general, quickly dismissing the question.

"Sir, we're just trying to figure out what's going on here. Craig and Kevin are both missing, and their sister's home was ransacked. She was also nearly run over by a vehicle today, and we don't believe that's coincidence."

"I'm sorry to hear that, really, I am, but Craig Ross has nothing to do with this. I'd stake my oak cluster on it."

"What's the name of the bar where the incident took place?" asked Ace.

"It's the Air Raid started by an ex-airborne guy. He doesn't take any shit and usually hires some of the kids in the unit to work as bouncers on their time off. According to Craig, his brother was drunk and out of control. Took a few swings at him and was finally restrained by a couple of patrons. He's not a very big guy. If you didn't know, they were all adopted. Craig is a decent size fella, maybe your size," he said, pointing at Ace. "Kevin is small, maybe five-feet-eight, a hundred-and-sixty-five pounds, maybe."

"Thank you, General." Blade stood, effectively ending the conversation, and turned toward the door for Ace to follow.

"If you boys need anything, just holler at me. I'm happy to help out if I can." Blade waited until they were safely back in the truck before speaking.

"What do you think?" he asked Ace.

"I think the general has some blind spots where it comes to Craig Ross. I'm not sure he has any involvement in this, but if they're as close as Willa said, it would seem he might have known what his brother was doing." Blade nodded.

"I feel like a drink."

CHAPTER TEN

Willa sat at the large round table inside the restaurant, waiting for someone to speak. The ice cubes floated in her soda, mimicking her own feelings of floating on a sheet of ice, grasping for anything in the sea of uncertainty.

Scott sat vigilantly to her side as if guarding over her, his big beefy body ready to defend if needed. She knew she was safe in this place, yet it seemed that all these men had an air of caution and protection around them.

"Willa, we asked you to meet with us to see if you could give us some more information about your brothers," said Ghost. The intensity of his stare made Willa squirm slightly in her seat. Skull was bigger than this man, but not by much. He was large and possessed a wisdom in his face and eyes that Skull did not. He seemed dangerous and yet not, all at the same time.

"Of course, anything you need," she said, nodding. "As I said before, I don't know anything about what either of them do in the Army, but I know they both enjoyed being in the service, or, at least, I think they did." Ghost eyed the woman cautiously and looked toward Skull.

"One question before we get started, honey," said Ghost, "were you aware of who the Steel Patriots MC were before coming up to the garage that day? It won't matter to us either way, Willa." Willa's face blanched, the pale skin nearly translucent in the light of the restaurant.

"Yes," she whispered. Ghost nodded. "I-I asked the sheriff if there was anyone who might be able to help me, and he said I should come up here. I was going to come and see the bike anyway; I swear to you I was coming this way. When he said you might help me find my brothers, I-I'm sorry I didn't tell you."

"It's okay," said Ghost, nodding. "Just understand that's the last time. Going forward, we're completely transparent; us to you and you to us. Understood?" She nodded, feeling the tears rising within her but pushing them back in place.

"Willa," Skull said softly, "our teammates who went down to Bragg said that according to General Donan, your brother Kevin is a bit of a…"

"A what?" she asked defensively.

"A fuckup," said Gunner quickly. All eyes turned to him, glaring. "What? Stop pussy footing around. She needs to know the truth if we're going to get to the truth of what happened to them."

"A fuckup? He said that Kevin was a fuckup?" she asked. Gunner nodded, and as she scanned each man's face, they all nodded in her direction. "I see. I honestly don't know what to say about that. Kevin was always the most responsible of all of us, even me. He joined the Army because he wanted to be just like Craig. He said… he told me he loved it. I had no idea…"

"What about Craig? Did he love it?" asked Ghost.

"Yes, I mean, I think he did. Geez, I really don't know much at all, do I?" Willa looked down at her folded hands in her lap, twisting her fingers nervously. "I was so wrapped up in my own business, developing my software, I guess I didn't really notice the changes in them until it was too late."

"Changes?" asked Skull. "What do you mean?"

"Before this last time when I saw them a few weeks ago, it had been months. We talked all the time, but I just didn't get out this way a lot from the west coast, and one or both was usually deployed somewhere. They just didn't talk to me like they usually did. We were always really open with one another, but they seemed less so these last few months. I assumed it was something they were doing with the military."

CHAPTER ELEVEN

Ace and Blade walked into the dimly lit bar, their eyes adjusting to the lack of light, the scent of stale beer and sweat filling their nostrils. Dozens of young soldiers, although none in uniform, filled the space. Both men recognized the carriage of the bar full of military men, the buzz-cut hair, the stiff spines, and the cautious glances toward the newcomers entering the bar.

Ace didn't stick out much from the others, but Blade, with his muscled body and long hair, was definitely a stand-out. He nodded toward two empty stools at the end of the bar, giving Ace the one at the very end. Although he was much better around people than he'd been prior to marrying Charlie, he was still a bit withdrawn in crowds of new people.

"Is it just me, or do the women in here look like high school girls?" asked Ace, glancing around the bar.

"It's not you. They don't look old enough to drive, let alone drink," said Blade. Two cardboard coasters were slapped on the bar in front of them.

"You fuckin' cops?" asked the bartender.

"Nope. You concerned about cops being in here?" Blade gave the other man a hard stare. He was tall and wiry, his thinning hair and beard giving way to a wrinkled face.

"Everyone gets checked in here. Girls just look young is all. What'll it be?"

"Beer," said Ace.

"Whiskey," said Blade. He looked toward the crowd once more and noticed a group of young soldiers seated at a round table, laughing and clinking glasses every few seconds. Two young girls with skirts too short, tops too low, and common sense non-existent approached the table, seductively leaning forward. Blade shook his head at the spectacle and then reminded himself that once upon a time, he was one of those young soldiers with shit for brains and an overactive dick.

"Here you go. That'll be ten bucks." Ace slid a twenty across the bar.

"Keep the change," he said. The bartender eyed him suspiciously and then leaned forward, his bony elbows propped on the sticky surface of the old wood bar.

"What do you fellas want?"

"You here the night of the bar fight?" asked Blade.

"You're gonna have to be more specific than that," chuckled the older man.

"Right," huffed Blade, "it was two brothers. One Asian and one black."

"The Ross brothers?" Ace and Blade nodded. "Yea, I was here, but that sure wasn't their first fight."

"What do you mean?" said Ace, leaning closer.

"No need to invade my space, son. Anyone in here will tell you the Ross brothers routinely get into it here and everywhere else. Those boys like to fight more than they like to eat, drink, or fuck," he laughed.

"What do they fight about?" asked Blade.

"Everything... anything," he chuffed again. "Few months ago, it was the boy gettin' all riled cause his brother had him transferred here without his knowledge. Said he just wanted to help him, keep an eye on him. The young one, Kellen..."

"Kevin," said Ace.

"Were you aware that they were both at Bragg now?" Whiskey could tell by her expression that she wasn't aware of it and continued. "General Donan said that Kevin was a supply specialist."

"A supply specialist? I don't know. I mean, do supply specialists get sent overseas?" she asked the table.

"Yes. I mean, supplies are still needed and distributed at bases overseas, so technically, yes. Plus, they do a lot more than just manage supplies," said Whiskey. "What were they like, these last few months when you visited?"

"They both knew that after selling my software design that I was going to move closer to them. With Craig retiring, I really wanted to be closer, you know, like it was before. Craig, well, you know the story. Mom and Dad died, and he was pretty much forced into taking care of us. Kevin and I were both good kids. He ran cross-country, and I was in cheerleading and gymnastics. Craig did everything he could to make sure we had the opportunity to participate in whatever we wanted."

"Admirable for someone so young himself," said Ghost. "Did he date? Marry?" She shook her head, the long blonde curls swishing across her back, brushing against Skull's arm. A flash of heat raced up his extremity, and he groaned.

"Very little. I mean, not that I saw anyway. He never brought a woman home, but I know for a fact he dated a few. When I left for college, Kevin was entering his junior year of high school. I thought everything was fine and felt good that Craig would soon be able to do whatever he wanted instead of being mother and father to us."

"Kevin didn't want to go to college?" asked Zulu.

"No, his grades were okay, but they weren't good enough for college. Besides, he always knew he would follow Craig. He was his hero." Looks were exchanged around the table, and Ghost stood, circling the table.

"When they helped you move into your apartment, did they say anything at all?" asked Ghost.

"No, but I definitely noticed that they were behaving strangely. Kevin kept looking out the apartment window like he was waiting for someone. When I asked them why they were so late, they said they didn't get to leave North Carolina on time, but I know that was a lie."

"Why did you know it was a lie?" asked Skull.

"We all have trackers on our phones to know where we are in the world. When they were deployed, they would turn it off, but in the states, they would turn it back on, and we all knew where the others were at. Craig insisted. I watched them leave Fayetteville at four a.m. That meant they should have been to me by ten, maybe noon at the latest, but they didn't arrive until nearly five."

"Did they give you a reason?" asked Skull.

"No, they just said they got delayed and changed the subject. Honestly, I was just so happy to see them both and finally be living closer; I just let it go. I was nearly done with all the unpacking when they got there. They moved my bigger pieces of furniture around for me, but I could tell they were in a hurry. Around seven or eight, they said they had to leave to get back to Bragg but promised we would meet up the following weekend."

"And did you?" asked Ghost.

"No, they called and said they both had duty and wouldn't be able to come up. I was disappointed, but I understood. That's about the time when I started feeling like someone was watching me. I never saw anyone, but it was just that feeling you get when you're in the grocery store and the hairs on the back of your neck rise, or when I was walking down the street, I felt like someone was following me. The morning I left for the store, I really felt it strongly. I practically ran from the apartment to the car. Then, well, you know what happened after that. I returned to find the mess in my apartment, called the sheriff, they took the report, and that's it."

"Did either of your brothers leave anything for you when they were there? Did they leave a package or anything?" Willa shook her head, then stopped, nibbling on her lower lip.

"Willa? Was there something?" asked Skull.

"Nothing they left for me, but Kevin asked to use my computer to check his e-mail. I didn't remember that until just now. Craig ran across the street to pick up pizza and soda for us, and the minute he left, Kevin asked to use the computer."

"Do you have your computer?" asked Ghost.

"Yes, right here. I keep it with me almost everywhere I go because I'm always getting ideas on how to improve the software I'm working on or ideas for something new." She pulled the laptop out of her bag and fired it up. The men moved their chairs or bodies to position behind her, watching as she logged in, checking her history.

"This is strange," she said, looking at the screen, "it doesn't show that he was checking mail at all. In fact, he never even logged into the internet."

"Is there any other way he could have checked it?" asked Skull.

"No, but it looks like he downloaded something to my computer. This folder here, *E&HR*."

"E&HR? Any idea what that could mean?" asked Ghost.

"Maybe. Our parents' names were Edward and Helen Ross. If he thought this was important, he might use those initials, hoping I would recognize it." She tried clicking on the file several times. "I can't open the file. It has a passcode, and I don't know what that is."

"Can we run an encryption program?" asked Whiskey. All eyes turned toward him, and he shrugged. "What? I've been listening to Ace."

"We can, but I'd have to build one. It's not really my expertise, and it might harm the file. This looks complicated to me. Maybe we could take it to someone?"

"Ace should be back in a day or so. We'll wait for him, but for now, don't let that laptop out of your sight," said Ghost. "Skull? Stay by her side. Any jobs you're currently doing, give them to Whiskey, Razor, or Tango unless she's with you in the garage. Willa? I know it's hard, honey, but we need you to stay within the confines of our property. If your brothers try to call you, let us know about it but don't answer the calls."

"Of course, but one last thing. After my brothers left and I didn't hear from them for a few days, I tracked their phones. I couldn't find Craig's, but Kevin's was listed as somewhere off the coast of Florida."

"On an island?" asked Skull.

"No. Like literally in the middle of the Atlantic. I logged onto a GPS system to see where the coordinates were, and it was in the middle of the water, no islands, nothing." Ghost let out a long slow breath, raking his fingers through the thick salt and pepper hair.

"Fucking hell."

"Yea, right, Kevin, he was some kinda pissed off. Screamed at his brother. Said he was gonna get them both killed or some shit. That older one, he sure knew how to push his buttons. Couldn't ever hear much of what he was saying. Usually, he'd just laugh at the younger one and shove him a time or two, like he was trying to get in a fight with him."

"What started this last fight?" asked Blade.

"Not sure. Didn't ask. Took five boys to break it up, though. The young one, he's smaller than his brother, but he's damned sure a fine fighter. Knows all them karate moves and such." The bartender lifted his head, looking around the room. "There, them two boys in the corner over there. They were here that night and pulled 'em apart."

"Thanks," said Blade, standing to move toward the back of the room. Ace started to follow, but the bartender gripped his arm, causing Ace to pull away quicker than he intended.

"Ain't tryin' to kiss you, son. Tell your buddy they ain't just any boys. Those are Rangers. He needs to watch his ass." Ace grinned at the man and nodded.

"I'll be sure and tell my friend, the Green Beret, you're concerned for him." The old man opened and closed his mouth a few times as Ace walked away, following Blade to the table.

The two men at the table slowly raised their heads to meet Blade's dark eyes. It was as if they knew he was one of them, Special Forces.

"Brother," said the shorter man, his dark blonde hair touching the tips of his collar.

"Brothers. Name's Blade, and this is my friend Ace. We're helping a friend find her brothers, and according to the bartender, you two helped break up a fight between them a few weeks ago."

"I'm Wojo, and this is Dud. Yea, that was us. Craig Ross. Didn't know the other guy was his brother. I mean, Ross is black, and the other guy was little and Asian. He was wiry and skilled in martial arts, that's for damn sure. I still have a bruise from one of the kicks he landed."

"Did you hear what they were arguing about?"

"Not really. The little one just kept screaming that he was going to get them killed or something. Said he'd gone off the rails and was yelling that he put some woman in danger."

"A woman?" asked Ace, suddenly perking up and stepping into the conversation.

"Yea, Willa was the name. I only remember because it was an unusual name. When I asked the older guy who the woman was, he just shrugged his shoulders and said the other guy was drunk."

"Did he appear drunk?" asked Blade.

"Honestly? No. He seemed completely sane and sober, just pissed off at the other guy and worried about this chick Willa."

"Did the MPs question you?" asked Blade.

"MPs, sheriff, police, you name it, and they asked us questions. We don't know either of the guys involved, just happened to be here when the fight broke out."

"Who started it?" asked Ace.

"Definitely the bigger guy. He was mouthing off to his brother. I couldn't hear everything, but I'd catch a few words here and there like he was antagonizing him, saying things like 'little man' or 'pussy.' Shit like that. Little guy finally got pissed and gave him a roundhouse kick to the chest. Pretty fucking spectacular kick too."

"Anyone else with them?" asked Blade.

"Not that I saw. Little one was already here at the bar when the other one came in and started his shit. Problem was, he never threw a punch. Let the other guy do all the fighting, which was why they hauled him off, not the big one."

Blade looked at Ace, letting out a long slow breath. Standing, he shook hands with the other men and dropped his business card.

"If you think of anything else, give me a call." Nodding, they walked away and out into the parking lot. "I don't like this."

"Agree. I think the older brother intentionally started the fight. Question is, why? I mean, if Kevin was worried for Willa, but Craig wasn't, what does that say?"

"Not sure, brother, but I think we need to get back to Virginia and speak to Skull and Ghost."

"Happy to hear that," said Ace, grinning. Blade stared at him a minute, and he spoke again. "I miss my wife, Blade. I never thought I'd utter those words, but damn, I miss Charlie. She's my everything." Blade gave a sideways grin to his friend.

"Fucking awesome, brother, fucking awesome."

CHAPTER TWELVE

"So, the cottage has everything you need. We stocked the refrigerator for you, and the beds are clean with fresh linens. It's still behind the gates, so it's secure. No one can get to you here." Skull stood in the middle of the living room with his hands in his pockets, just turning slightly every now and then, nodding toward something and then turning back to face Willa.

"It's lovely, really. Thank you for this, Scott."

"It's no problem, Willa, really. We'll find your brothers. In the meantime, if you need me, just call. My phone number is on the counter."

"You're leaving?" she shrieked.

"Uh, well, yea, that was the plan. I mean, I don't live here in the cottage."

"Right." Willa swallowed hard and then looked back up at Skull. She could feel the emotions bubbling to the surface again and willed herself to maintain control.

"Hey, hey, Willa, it's okay. I can stay in the other bedroom if that makes you feel more comfortable." Skull took a step toward the tiny woman, her head popping up to stare into his face. Her big green eyes shined with the unshed tears. Fear was oozing off her little body, and that made him angry.

"I'm sorry, Scott. It's just that I'm scared. I'm scared and confused, and I know you said this place is secure and safe, but... but I just don't feel very safe right now." He nodded and moved toward the bar stool. Seated, he was still much taller than she was, but at least lower and closer to looking eye to eye.

"Listen, Willa, I know that we don't know one another very well, but know this, I would never allow a woman to feel unsafe while I'm around. If you're scared, just tell me. If you're hungry, tell me. If I can fix it, I will. It's really that simple." She nodded, wiping the tears from her cheeks.

"Thank you, Scott. I'm sorry to be so needy. I just don't understand what's going on. Why would the phone signal be right in the middle of the Atlantic? Why would they just disappear without telling me? None of this makes sense." Her fear was leading to frustration and a bit of panic.

Skull reached out for her hand, his rough callused fingers sliding down her arm. Everything about her seemed so delicate and tiny. He could wrap his hand around her upper arm, and his fingers would overlap.

"As long as I'm here, Willa, you won't ever have to feel afraid. If you want to go down to Florida and see if we can find your brothers, we'll do that." He pulled her closer, and she willingly leaned into his chest, wrapping her arms around his waist. He could feel her take in a deep breath, inhaling the scent of his shirt.

"You smell nice," she whispered. Skull lay one big hand on her back and pressed her forward into his body.

"So do you, Willa." His voice was brusque and rough. Willa pulled back, looking up into his face. Laying her fingers against the roughness of his beard, she let them dance down the long line of the scar. With her other hand, she shoved back the dark brown hair falling over his eyes.

"Why do you keep the beard and your hair so long? Is it to cover the scar?" Her warm breath scorched the skin at his throat, and he swallowed hard, pulling back to look down into the emerald orbs.

"Partly. I mean, yea. The scar is ugly, and people stare at it. I just try to cover it up as much as I can."

"It's not ugly, Scott. It's part of you. It says you were brave and did something incredibly dangerous to protect the rest of us. I think that's amazing." Willa's delicate fingers touched his scar with the lightness of a butterfly's wings. Tracing the line of the scar, she followed along to the seam of his lips and leaned forward, pressing her own against his gently.

Scott was so shocked by her actions, he could barely think. His hands still lay gently at her small waist, her body safely encased between his thick muscular thighs. The kiss was sweet and innocent at first, and then he felt the wetness of her tongue gliding along his lips. He had no choice. Opening his mouth, he gladly accepted her tongue, tasting her, inhaling her.

Willa let her arms wrap around his neck, the heat of his wide hands resting just above her waistband. She felt it the moment he gave in and opened for her, allowing her to taste him fully and take what she'd wanted since the moment she saw him. As she felt the fire build within her, she also felt Scott's body react, the stiff rod between his legs now pressing against her stomach, almost making panic bubble within her.

It was as if he read her mind, pulling back breathlessly.

"Willa," he panted, leaning his forehead against hers, "Willa, honey, I think we should slow down. You're scared and vulnerable right now. I don't want to take advantage of you."

"In case you missed it, Scott, I made the first move, not you. I was kind of tired of waiting on you," she grinned. That brought out a small chuckle as he stood, carefully adjusting himself and blushing.

"Still, I think we just need a moment. I'll run to the barn and grab some clothes and get some dinner for us. I'll be back in about thirty minutes. That will give you time to unpack and shower or do whatever you need to do. Don't open the door for anyone except me or one of the Patriots. Okay?"

"Aye, aye, captain," she said, grinning with a mock salute.

"Funny, very funny." Skull turned toward the door and then walked back to where Willa stood, kissing her forehead. "Stay inside." She nodded once again, locking the door as he left.

Several minutes later, she was still standing at the door, staring at it as if hoping he'd come back. Stepping away, she let out a long slow breath, touching her lips. The heat in her belly was not deteriorating the way she'd hoped. In fact, the more she thought about staying in the cottage alone with Scott, the more the fire flamed.

"What are you going to do now, Willa?"

CHAPTER THIRTEEN

"I want to talk to Lt. Schumer before we leave," said Blade as they shoved their bags into the back of the car.

"Schumer? The guy who was arguing with General Donan? Why?" Ace normally didn't question Blade's methods, but this seemed unnecessary.

"Something Donan said. He said they were arguing over the Ross brothers and the disappearance of the cargo. Maybe Schumer doesn't have the same affinity toward Craig Ross." Ace nodded as he followed Blade toward Schumer's office. Tapping on the door, Blade ducked his head in to see Schumer reading through piles of paperwork.

"Can I help you?" the man asked.

"Lt. Schumer, we met briefly in the general's office the other day," said Blade. The other man eyed him suspiciously but nodded for him to have a seat, Ace following suit. "The general said you two were in disagreement about the missing shipments."

"You got that right, but I'm sorry, I don't have the authority to discuss this with you, and you don't have the clearance, or do you?" he said, staring at the two men. Ace grinned at the man but said nothing.

"We have higher clearance than you, lieutenant, but that's not important. We think Craig Ross may be more involved in this than the general wants to admit. I have no doubt that Kevin Ross wasn't exactly the perfect soldier, but…" Schumer held up his hand and stopped Blade.

"That's where you're wrong," he said softly. Standing, he moved to close the door and then sat back down, leaning forward in his chair. He continued in a low voice.

"What do you mean?" asked Ace.

"Kevin Ross is not a fuck up. He was a perfect soldier until his brother started coming around him more, interfering in his duty stations, his assignments. It all started to be too much for Kevin, and he started fighting back."

"Wait, the records say he was busted down in rank, drunk and disorderly…"

"Yea, yea, I know what the records say, but I also know that Kevin Ross never took a drink in his life. That arrest, the one with the D&O charge? A sobriety test was never performed, nor did they do an alcohol level test."

"Then how did he get charged?" asked Blade. Schumer just stared at him.

"Any time Kevin was in trouble, Craig was around. I worked with Kevin at Andrews and was deployed with him. He was a stellar soldier. Followed the rules, always on time, always lending a hand to a fellow soldier. He was totally devoted to his sister. The guy never, and I do mean never, broke the rules. Suddenly, Craig is around, and Kevin's getting into all sorts of shit, according to Donan. I don't buy it for a fucking minute."

"So, you think Craig and Donan are in on something?" asked Blade.

"I didn't say that," Schumer said, throwing his hands up in defense. "I'm saying all this blame laid at Kevin's feet seems too convenient. Everything he's being accused of is ridiculous."

"What about all the missing shipments and that he was on duty when they happened?"

"Yea, so was Craig and a half dozen other guys. Craig isn't in supply, but for some strange reason, every time one of those shipments came in, Craig was working night duty. He's a career man who can be home by five o'clock every night. Why in the hell would he be on night duty?"

"Why indeed," said Blade.

"Look, I can't say anything else, but I don't believe for one damned minute that if anything is going on that Craig isn't involved in this too. Kevin was pissed at his brother, really pissed about something. I walked in on them arguing in the warehouse. They were in a back corner whispering shit, and I heard Kevin tell his brother that whatever he'd done, he'd just signed the death warrant for their sister, Willa."

"Fuuuuck," groaned Blade.

"What?" said Schumer.

"We know her. She came to our team for help in finding her brothers."

"Well, wherever she is, I hope you can protect her. Something is rotten here, and I have no clue what or who all is behind it. Kevin is a good man and would never do anything to put his brother or sister in harm's way." Ace eyed the man up and down, looking around the office. There were no photos of any family members, no personal mementos. Schumer was easily thirty to thirty-five years old and what most women would describe as good-looking.

"You're in love," he said casually.

"What!? That's ridiculous! I have no one in my life right now," said Schumer, standing.

"I'm not judging," said Ace. "You're in love with Kevin, and Craig disapproved, and I suspect, so does General Donan." Schumer's face was now perspiring, his eyes wide with panic.

"Brother, we truly don't give a shit. We're just trying to help find Kevin and Craig." Blade leaned against a bookshelf, his arms folded across his chest, the dark hair hanging over one eye. He watched as Schumer swallowed hard, returning to his seat.

"We-we met at Ramstad. I was working as an aid to Donan, and Kevin was preparing troops for deployment. We were just friends at first, you know, movies, dinner, that kind of shit. Then one night, we got to talking about the fact that neither of us had a woman in our lives, and, well, one thing led to another. That was six years ago. We're in love and hope to be married one day."

"So why all the subterfuge?" asked Ace. "I mean, the military has a policy now…"

"Policy? It's such bullshit! Donan found out about us, I'm pretty damned sure, through Craig. Basically, he has me by the balls for at least another year. Craig told Kevin he could make my life and my career a living hell if he didn't do what he asked him to do."

"And what did he ask him to do?" asked Blade.

"I don't know. Honestly, I have no idea. Kevin didn't want me involved. He said we needed to stay apart as much as possible. He even tried to convince Craig that we weren't a couple anymore, but he didn't buy it."

"I don't get it," said Ace. "Why do all this to his brother? Was Craig stealing the weapons and ammunition? If so, why?"

"I wish I could answer that, but as I said, Kevin wouldn't tell me anything. He said it was better if I knew nothing. I can tell you that after they got back from helping their sister move her things, he was really worried about her safety. He said Craig didn't care who he hurt, including Willa. Kevin was pretty sure that his brother had men watching her."

Blade let out a long slow breath and circled the room, pushing his fingers through his dark hair. Ace let the facts filter through his mind, trying to categorize and prioritize each one in order to recall it when it was needed.

"Can you tell us anything else?" asked Blade.

"I wish I could, but there's nothing else to tell. I'd offer my help, but Donan is watching me like a hawk. If I do anything out of the norm, he'll have me busted so low, I'll never crawl out. Honestly, I don't give a shit. I just want Kevin found, safe, and unharmed."

"We'll do our best," said Blade, reaching into his pocket. He placed a business card in the other man's hand and nodded, leaving the office.

"How did you know?" asked Schumer, staring at Ace. Ace smirked and shrugged his shoulders.

"No pictures of a wife or kids, but you have the look of a man in love. I know that look. It just seemed to fit. You were pretty concerned for Kevin, and it felt beyond that of friendship. It's all good, brother. Believe me, we really don't give a shit. We'll find him for you, and Craig."

"When you find Craig, I'd like to have a little chat with him." Ace grinned and followed Blade down the long hallway once again. Inside their vehicle, neither man said anything as they pulled away from the massive base.

It was an hour later before Blade finally spoke.

"Fucked. Up. Shit."

CHAPTER FOURTEEN

Skull bounded down the steps of the barn with a backpack slung over his shoulder and walked toward the kitchen. George and Mary were busy with their nightly routine of preparing meals for the restaurant, alongside several part-time members of the restaurant staff.

"Hey, George, hi, Mary," he said, smiling at the older couple. Mary turned with a big grin and wrapped him in a hug, kissing his cheek.

"What can I get you to eat, honey?"

"Actually, I'm staying with a new guest of ours, Willa Ross, at the cottage." George snapped to attention and turned quickly, staring at Skull. Skull held up both hands, shaking his head at the older man. "It's not like that, George. She needs our protection, and she's scared to stay in the cottage by herself. I just came to get a change of clothes and pick up something for dinner."

"Uh huh," he said, nodding his head at the big man. "And you're just gonna sleep on the sofa and protect her?"

"No, I mean, yes, no, there's an extra room in the cottage. You know that," he said, shuffling his feet.

"George! Leave him alone," said Mary. "I think it's sweet of you, Skull. You're a fine young man, and you deserve to find a good woman. If this is just protection, then that's fine. If not, then, well, we'll all be anxious to watch it happen and get to know her."

"It's not! Never mind, can I just get something to go for the two of us?" he said, flustered.

"Yep," said George. "Here, I just pulled out a pizza. Ought to be big enough for the two of you. Skull? You're a fine man. One I'm proud to think of as a son, just do you."

"Thanks, George," he said, grabbing the pizza box. "See ya later, Mary."

"See ya later, honey. Oh, and Skull?"

"Yea?"

"Just be you, baby," she said, grinning at the big man. "You're enough. Just be you." Skull grinned at the older woman and nodded.

Mary and George, although living together as a couple, had decided not to get married at their ages. George had been married years ago while serving in the military, but when his first wife died, he spiraled without a purpose. When he came to work for the Steel Patriots, he became a solid fixture for the team and helped guide them in many ways, often acting like the wise old father or grandfather.

Mary was hired by the women to help with the children initially, although every one of them knew she and George would hit it off, and so they did.

"You like that boy, don't you?" said George, kissing Mary's temple.

"I do," she smiled. "He's got a pain inside him that I can't quite figure out, and yet there's this tender sweetness to him. I just think he needs the right person to make all that settle and come out alright… like mixing a cake… you know what I mean?"

"Woman, I never know what you mean, but I still love you," he said, kissing her again.

"Oh you!" she laughed. "How about I show you what I mean later?"

"Now that is an order I'll take all day long."

Skull wound his way along the pathway toward the cottage, listening to the sharp sounds of the night, the floating notes of music coming from the restaurant, the call of an owl in the distance. As he approached the cottage, his heart started to beat faster, sweat beading at the back of his neck. He wasn't sure why he was so nervous, but for some reason, he was.

Before he could even knock on the door, Willa swung it open and smiled up at him.

"Hi," she said, standing in the cutest little pajamas he'd ever seen. They were simple and conservative, long pants and a button-up top covered in pink ice cream cones.

"You opened the door." It came out much harsher than he intended, but damnit, he was concerned for her safety, and opening the door to just anyone might get her killed.

"I did." Willa placed her hands at her hips defensively, nearly making Skull laugh at the absurdity of her believing she might frighten or intimidate anyone away.

"You shouldn't open the door unless you know who it is," he snarled.

"I did know who it was," she said, staring up at him. "I saw you coming down the path and knew your hands were full."

"Oh." Skull lowered his head in embarrassment and stepped around her, placing the pizza on the counter. "Which room did you choose?" Willa frowned at him. It was as if all their progress was thrown out the window, his harsh, biting retorts returning to the surface.

"The one back there," she said, pointing behind her. Skull nodded and moved toward the other bedroom, setting his backpack on the bed. He let out a long slow sigh and realized he'd acted like an asshole. Walking back toward the kitchen with every intention of apologizing, he didn't see Willa. Thinking she'd gone to the restroom, he got out plates and napkins for the pizza and pulled out two bottled waters.

He waited patiently at the table, and when she didn't return, he walked toward her bedroom, knocking on the door.

"Willa?"

"What?" she said harshly.

"Aren't you hungry? I've got pizza."

"No thanks. Not hungry anymore. I'm just tired." He could hear her sniffle and cursed himself.

"Willa, I'm sorry if I sounded mean, but I'm trying to protect you." He waited patiently, hearing nothing on the other side of the door. "Okay, okay, I'll just be out here if you need anything."

As he started toward the kitchen once again, he heard the bedroom door open, violently slamming against the wall.

"You know what, Scott. I'm tired of your moody unpredictable behavior! I've done everything I know to do to get you to understand that I'm interested in you. I've tried to talk to you, but noooo, you don't like to talk! I've tried to be nice to you, but noooo, being nice isn't in your repertoire. I even made the first damn move! I. Kissed. You!" she said, walking closer and poking his big chest with her tiny finger at the emphasis of every word.

"I'm so humiliated right now! I'm so..." Her words were cut off by his lips slamming against hers as he pressed her against the door, his big body crushing her. Lifting her easily, he wrapped her legs around his waist, driving his hands into her hair, devouring her mouth. He ground his thick cock into her crotch, her eyes flying open. It was exactly the effect he wanted.

"I'm sorry," he said, pulling back, leaning his forehead against hers. "I don't mean to be unpredictable and moody. I'm not pushing you away, Willa. I'm concerned for your safety, and I guess I'm not doing a very good job of showing you that."

"I don't understand what's happening," she said, wrapping her arms around his neck.

"I don't understand it either, but it seems to happen a lot around here," he laughed. "Listen, Willa, all I know is I like you more than any woman I've ever met. If you're willing to risk your toes being around me, I do want to see what happens between us. But hear me loud and clear. Your safety is my number one priority. If I feel as though I can't focus because of our personal relationship, I'll ask one of the other brothers to step in."

Willa looked concerned with that for a moment but then gently nodded her head.

"I need to hear you say you understand. I need you to say it, Willa."

"Yes. Yes, I want to pursue a relationship with you while you're keeping me safe. Yes, I understand that my safety is your number one priority. Yes, I understand that if at any time you feel distracted, you might ask one of the others to watch over me. And yes, I'm more than willing to risk my toes for you, Scott Crawford."

"You do like your words, don't you?" he smiled. Willa laughed, kissing him once more. "Come on, woman. I'm hungry."

Skull was surprised to see Willa eat four slices of pizza. For someone so small, she certainly had an appetite. By the time the plates were cleared and the trash disposed of, they were both tired but settled on the sofa to watch a movie.

"This is really a lovely cottage," she said, looking around the room. "I like how warm and inviting the interior is. It's so different from the apartment I rented."

"It's a cool place. You met Tinley earlier." Willa nodded. "Her daughter, Keegan, and another brother, Hawk, stayed here a few months back. It's where they fell in love." Willa noticed the blush on his cheeks and smiled, leaning her head against his shoulder. They were both silent for several minutes, and then she finally asked what had been plaguing her mind.

"Did your friends learn anything about my brothers?" she asked. Skull knew that Blade and Ace learned a great deal at Bragg, but he wasn't prepared to tell Willa anything until they were back.

"We'll know tomorrow. They should be back by around noon." She simply nodded, and Skull looked down at her. "No matter what, Willa, I'm here for you."

Looking up into his eyes, Willa felt the familiar tug in her gut, the need to feel this man by her side. She'd never been shy about asking for what she wanted. When you're small, sometimes you need to be loud to get people to hear you, both in voice and body. Willa knew what she wanted, and she wasn't about to just walk away from it.

"Thank you, Scott. Do you... do you think you would be okay sleeping with me tonight?" Scott shifted slightly in the seat. He was more than okay with it, but he worried that Willa would be a bit surprised by how much space he took up, everywhere.

"I'm more than happy to lie with you, Willa, but you control everything. Understand?"

"You're a surprise in every way, Scott. You're this big bear of a man with a gruff exterior that says, 'back off.' Yet there's this softer, sweeter inner part of you. A well-educated, thoughtful, kind man that acts as if he hasn't lived in the outside world in decades." He nodded thoughtfully.

"I supposed that's partly true," he said, looking down at her. "I mean, I was in the service for nearly thirteen years and then immediately came to work for Steel Patriots, which is run like a military organization. I've always been aware of how my size affects those around me, and I guess I've just learned to try and stand back and be a little quieter."

"Well, I like all of you, Scott. Truly."

Willa stood slowly and reached out her hand, extending it to the big man seated in front of her. Skull wrapped his big fingers around her delicate ones, standing to tower above her, and followed her toward the bedroom. Moving to the opposite side of the bed, he watched as she slowly unbuttoned her pajama top, the soft cotton falling from her body.

She was exactly as he'd pictured. Small pert breasts perched on a lean upper body, her muscles defined and toned. The long waves of blonde hair covered her back, one lone strand falling over her shoulder, the tip gently brushing against one erect nipple. Her eyes never left his, even as he felt himself growing harder. Sliding her thumbs under the waistband, she pushed the pajama pants down, stepping out of them, her naked body now fully exposed to him. Standing nervously, literally bared to him, Willa just let him take her in, her hands opening and closing at her sides.

"Say something, Scott," she whispered.

"You're fucking beautiful," he said, taking a step forward. He toed off his boots and kicked them to the side, then pulled his socks off.

Willa was immediately struck by how big his feet were but also how sexy they were. His feet were literally sexy. Strong veins covered the tops of them, his nails neatly trimmed and clean. She wanted to giggle at the thought of him getting pedicures, but that's exactly what it looked like.

Pulling his shirt over his head, she sucked in a breath seeing the small scars over his chest. The scar on his face might be the most visible and largest, but he was littered with much smaller ones all over his body. His thick muscles rippled with every movement and breath. He reminded her of a famous professional wrestler, and she could feel herself blushing, the wetness building between her legs.

Willa desperately wanted to touch him but knew that if she did, he might leave her standing in the room by herself.

Unbuckling his jeans, Skull let them fall to the floor, his boxer briefs quickly following. He watched Willa's face for a reaction as he stood to his full erect height, literally, and grinned as she blushed and smiled at him.

"You really are big all over," she whispered. Skull chuckled.

"Yea, baby, I really am. We can stop, Willa, at any time, you say stop, and I'll stop. I'm a man. I have needs, but I'm not an animal. I'll never take you against your will. Although I'll tell you, I damn sure don't want to stop. You're beautiful, honey, so fucking beautiful," he said, stepping toward her, his big arms reaching out and pulling her against his body.

Willa wrapped her arms around him, feeling the safety and security of his steely arms, caging her against the strength of his chest. She inhaled his scent and smiled, kissing him just above each nipple.

"You're so perfect, Scott. I'm not afraid. Not of you. I'm afraid of this, afraid of what's happening between us. I'm afraid of what's happening with my brothers, but not you."

"Let's not talk about your brothers when we're naked in the bedroom, baby," he grinned. She giggled, and Skull pulled back the covers on the bed. He slid between the sheets and welcomed her into his arms. Truth be told, he would have been happier than shit just to hold her all night against his bare body, but Willa had other plans for sure.

"I want you," she whispered against his lips.

"I want you too, baby. At your pace," he said. Willa lay against the big hairy chest, feeling the fine hairs tickle her breasts. It was one of the most erotic things she'd ever been exposed to. Who would have thought a man's chest hair could make her nipples so hard. Maybe not any man, just Scott.

Seating herself on top of him, she felt his massive cock poking at her and moaned, the wetness and heat building in her own body. For a moment, she wondered if she would be able to take him, but then somewhere inside of her, she knew they were meant for one another.

Scott's big hand gripped her hair, twisting and wrapping it around his fisted hand, and pulled her to him, tasting her, nibbling on those beautiful, full pink lips. One big hand squeezed her tiny breast as he moaned against her mouth. He felt her grip his cock, lifting herself, sliding him back and forth along her warm, wet opening, her juices flowing more freely, saturating her tight little hole.

"Oh wow," she whispered with a small gasp, "wow... that's... wow..." Skull chuckled at her as she lowered herself slowly onto him, taking him a little at a time, feeling him stretch her. The stinging and burning were nearly overwhelming, but the pleasure far outweighed the discomfort. Willa knew that if she could just get this first time over with, she would be good to go afterward.

"Fuck, baby," he groaned, glancing down at their joined bodies, "Willa, baby, you're taking me. All of me."

"You're damn right I am," she smiled. Skull looked down at her pretty pussy sliding down his thick, full cock and smiled. Gripping her hips, he froze.

"What?" she asked. "Why did you stop me?"

"I don't have a condom," he moaned. How could he have been so stupid as to not bring a condom? He'd never taken a woman without being wrapped up.

"I'm on the pill, Scott, and I haven't been with anyone in three years. I'm clean. I trust you."

"I'm clean too, baby, and I haven't been with anyone in almost a year and always used a condom," he smiled.

"Good, then where were we," she grinned. Scott flipped her to her back, spreading her legs wide to accommodate his big hips, marveling at the flexibility of his little gymnast. He slid a large hand down the inside of one toned, tight thigh and groaned.

"I believe," he said, kissing her passionately, "I was about to fuck you."

"Yep," she said in a sexy rumble, rolling her hips against him, "that's exactly... oh yea... right there... where we were." Scott moved carefully at first, and then his lust and desire took over, the animal inside filling him with a need like nothing he'd ever felt before.

Willa was everything he never knew he wanted or needed. She was smart, successful, beautiful as fuck, and, more than that, she fit his body like a glove. Her tiny limbs wrapped around him, pulling him in deeper, and he was more than happy to oblige.

"Fuck, baby. Please, Willa…" Sweat rolled down his face, the volcano inside him ready to blow.

"Yes, now! Now, Scott!" she yelled.

"Thank fuck!" Scott rammed into her body, filling her with his hot seed, his own body racked with shudders of satisfaction as hers shook in unison. "Holy hell, that was fucking great!" Willa giggled, her legs still wrapped around him.

"It was amazing, Scott," she whispered against his lips. "I've never felt like that before, never experienced a simultaneous orgasm. I want more." Scott looked shocked, staring down into her face. She could feel the twitch of his cock inside her, already hardening once again, grinning at her as she was already moving against him, her walls squeezing him, milking him of everything.

"Never let it be said that Scott Crawford disappointed a lady."

CHAPTER FIFTEEN

"Who did you send the file to?" he asked, jabbing the man in the cage. Between the thick bars, he shoved the long steel rod, pressing a button to release a sharp jolt of electricity. His screams filtered through the dark night, ocean air filling his senses, the distant sounds of waves lapping against a shore somewhere.

"I... told you," he moaned breathlessly, "I didn't send it to anyone."

"You've always been a pain in my ass, Kevin. Following me around like some sick puppy. Did you want to fuck me? Knowing I wasn't your biological brother, did you have romantic feelings for me?" Craig Ross knew the words would hurt his brother, but he really didn't give a damn anymore.

"You know that isn't true. You're sick, Craig—sick! I loved you. You were my brother. That's all. Just like Willa is our sister." Kevin curled on his side, pain and fatigue overtaking his body. He couldn't remember how long he'd been in the cage, couldn't remember what day it was, only that he'd been inside the small cell far longer than he should have been. Had it not rained excessively the last few nights, he wouldn't have had any fresh water at all. As it was, he was running on empty.

"It won't be long, and you'll be dead, Kevin. You could do this one thing, you know. One simple thing to help you and your sister. A few more days of no food and no water, and you'll be done for."

"I don't care," he moaned, "kill me. I don't care." Craig circled the cage where he'd placed his brother, the other two men watching from a distance as he'd asked.

"No? What about Willa? Do you care about her? Or Lt. Schuman? Fine looking officer he is." Craig smirked at his brother. "I heard through the grapevine that he has a nice long dick. Is that true?" Kevin pushed himself to a seated position, pain flowing through his body all the way to his toes.

"Don't… touch Willa or Adam. They know nothing, Craig, nothing. This is between you and me," he said, staring at his brother. If he were healthy and in an open environment, he could take his brother in hand-to-hand. He was trained in five martial arts disciplines and more than skilled enough to take down his brother.

"Interesting," smiled Craig. "You really do care for them, don't you? Then tell me where you sent the information."

"I've told you," he said through clenched teeth. "I sent it nowhere."

"Have it your way." Craig jammed the cattle prod through the cage, landing a solid hit at his ribs, the electricity so violent he lost control of what little he held within his stomach and bowels. It didn't matter. He lost consciousness as well, infuriating his brother further.

"Fuck!" he yelled.

"Now what?" said the voice of the man behind him.

"Now I need to find my sister."

CHAPTER SIXTEEN

Skull lay against the stark white sheet, one big muscled arm behind his head, the other securely wrapped around the little pixie snuggled into his side. They'd fucked three times last night. No, that wasn't right. He knew it. They'd made love. He knew what fucking felt like. Fucking felt like satisfaction for a few brief moments. Your bodies release of pent-up energy, stress, and endorphins. He tried to think of what happened with them last night as just fucking, but no matter what, he couldn't.

Willa Ross was like no other woman he'd ever been with. She was smart and successful, outspoken without being obnoxious, caring, and filled with concern for her siblings. But it wasn't just that. She was smaller, tinier in every way, but despite that, she'd taken him, all of him, and kept coming back for more. He knew she'd be tired and sore this morning, but that didn't prevent his morning wood from forming a nice little tent. He gently kissed the top of her head, inhaling the fragrance he now knew as her shampoo.

Today he'd have to tell her about her brothers. Tell her that they believed Craig was behind everything and maybe tell her something she didn't know; that Kevin was gay and in a relationship.

She squirmed against his side, one leg rising slowly against his own and then curving to lie between his thighs. He wanted to moan aloud at the sensations in his body, but he simply closed his eyes and drawing in a long, slow, deep breath. When her hand slid from his chest lower and lower, he knew she was awake.

"You're playing a dangerous game baby," he said in a gruff morning voice.

"I'm not playing any games, Scott. I hope you know that," she said, kissing his jaw, that sweet little pink tongue darting out to taste the saltiness of his skin.

"I do." He kissed her soundly and she let her hand fall to his stiff, thick cock.

"Willa," he gasped, "baby girl you have to be sore this morning. I'm a lot of man and you took me three times last night."

"I am," she grinned, "but I can be very creative when I need to be." For a moment Scott wasn't sure what she meant, his brain lacking a serious amount of blood flow and oxygen. Honestly, his head was spinning with the sensations of her fingers dancing over his body, gripping the hot flesh of his cock.

Running her tongue down his abdomen, she kissed both hips and then took the tip of him in her mouth. There was no way she could take all of him, but she could give enough pleasure simply by rubbing him and sucking at the same time.

Scott pushed back against the pillows a bit so he could look down at her perfect lips wrapped around the head of his cock. It was almost too much, the sensations of those soft lips, the hot tongue gliding over him. His hips involuntarily jerked upward toward her mouth and she grinned. Her small fingers gliding up and down his heavy shaft.

"Fuck... Willa..."

"Come for me," she whispered seductively. He could only nod. I mean, what the fuck was he supposed to do?

Willa's lips were soft and warm, her tongue dancing circles around his head; sliding down she gave a quick suck to each of his heavy balls and then ran her tongue back up, taking him in her mouth once again. When she let her own fingers dance against her pussy, Scott couldn't take it any longer.

"Fuck! Baby girl..." She felt the hot liquid hit the back of her throat and swallowed hard, just in time for the second burst to hit, filling her mouth with salty, sweetness. Sucking down the last drop, she carefully licked the tip of his head and sat back on her heels grinning down at him. His chest rising and falling in heavy breaths.

"I think you're trying to kill me," he growled, pulling her on top of his chest. Willa giggled, shaking her head.

"Nope. That would defeat all my grand plans for you, Scott."

"Grand plans?"

"Yep," she said, pushing back and heading toward the bathroom. "I'm going to shower. Care to join me?" He could only laugh as she wiggled her tight ass cheeks in his direction.

"I'm not sure that shower is big enough for both of us honey, it's barely big enough for me. Take yours and I'll use the other bathroom. We need to get dressed and head to breakfast. Blade and Ace are back, and we have some things to discuss."

Willa's face crashed into despair and Scott realized his mistake.

"It's okay honey, nothing horrible. We just need to talk." She nodded, giving him a weak smile. He heard the shower start and moved to the other bathroom to do the same. Twenty minutes later he was dressed and waiting for her in the living room.

Willa stepped out in a pair of jeans with frayed bottoms, the tight Aerosmith t-shirt showing off her small, defined muscles.

"Aerosmith?" he grinned.

"Yea, Aerosmith. I like rock and roll," she smiled. "Why? You don't like Aerosmith?"

"No, no that's not it at all. I guess I just sort of figured you more as a Backstreet Boys or N'Sync kind of girl." Willa laughed, standing on her toes to kiss his cheek. He still had to bend a few inches, but her warm lips sent shivers down his spine as always.

"Not hardly. I'm a rock and roll girl all the way."

"Let's go baby. Breakfast with everyone and then meet with the guys." As they walked toward the barn, Skull told her about each of the team members she hadn't met yet. He gave a brief synopsis of Grace's story and the other women but didn't go into great detail. He knew that every time a new woman came into their fold, the wives were great about filling them in.

Fuck!

He was actually thinking about Willa becoming part of their team... a part of his team. He'd never in his entire life considered having a woman by his side for longer than an hour. Now he was having trouble thinking of his life without Willa.

"Scott? Yoohoo... Scott?"

"Oh, sorry I was thinking of... something. What did you say?"

"I asked if you have any family other than the family here."

"Oh, yea. My folks live in rural Ohio. They're good hard-working people. Pops retired last year, and my mom is trying to convince him to move closer to me. I think she's hoping she'll live to see grandchildren one day."

"And will she?" grinned Willa.

"Oh... I... well..."

"It's okay Scott, I'm teasing you. Have you ever thought about kids?"

"Honestly?" he said, looking down at her he took a deep breath. "Before I met you, I would have said that I'd never have children. I know it might seem stupid after only a few days together, but I can tell you Willa that I could see myself having a family with you."

"Wow! You really know how to go from grunting to wooing in sixty seconds don't you." She giggled looking up at him and then, noticing his serious expression, kissed him. "I've thought of it too,

Scott. I've always wanted children. I think when you're adopted you hope that you'll be able to give the kind of family life to a child that you didn't have. I mean, my adoptive parents were amazing... great really, but I want to make sure my child knows that he or she is wanted, loved."

"I can see how that would make you feel that way. Did you ever consider adopting children since you're adopted?"

"Absolutely! I always said that if I couldn't have children of my own, I would adopt or if I was with someone willing to have a lot of children." Scott nodded.

"I was an only child. My folks gave me a great life, lots of opportunities and my Pops worked his ass off to give me what I needed. But I missed out on the whole sibling thing. I think I've learned more about that by being here with the Steel Patriots than anywhere. We all act a bit like natural brothers."

"I see that in every interaction you guys have. I think Kevin and I acted like siblings, but Craig... he was so much older, I think he always just sort of took on a surrogate parent role."

Opening the door to the barn, Skull walked in holding securely to Willa's hand. The room was filled with his teammates and their families, all waiting patiently for the duo to arrive. It was quiet for the briefest of moments as all eyes turned toward them.

Skull froze for a moment and then saw the smiles rippling across the faces of his family and friends. As a loud cheer broke out, complete with raucous applause he blushed furiously.

"Um, what did I miss?" asked Willa, holding tight to his big paw.

"Nothing. This is my asshole family," he grinned, "acting just like asshole siblings. Come on baby, I'll introduce you to everyone." Skull pulled her toward the long tables of people and began introducing her to all the team members and then their wives. When he reached Grace with a baby on her hip and one in a highchair, Willa smiled wide.

"There are so many children!"

"We seem to be reproducing at an alarming rate," said Grace. "Although this is it for me and Ghost. Two is our limit."

"Fuck right it is," he growled. "I haven't had a decent nights' sleep in almost two years now."

"And you love it," said Grace, kissing her husband passionately. He let a small grin slip from his lips and nodded.

Damn straight he loved it. He'd waited years to find the right woman and Grace stumbled across his path, literally in the worst of circumstances. Their love was born of patience and fate.

"Have a seat Willa," said Tinley, rubbing her big belly. Willa took the seat next to the woman and then noticed the big, muscled man next to her and an identical one across the table. He looked a little younger than her, but not by much. She knew that her daughter was married to her husbands' twin, but she was having trouble computing the age differences.

"You're trying to figure out if I'm the better-looking twin," said the man seated across from her. Willa blushed.

"Ignore the asshole," said Skull. "That's Hawk. He's married to Keegan, Tinley's daughter. The one next to her, is Eagle."

"Hawk and Eagle?" she asked inquisitively.

"Yep beautiful," said Hawk as Skull gave him a threatening stare. "Sorry big man, relax. Remember we're all married here... happily. We were both Marine snipers, Willa."

"Then the names make perfect sense," she grinned.

"Everyone always tries to figure our little family out," said Tinley. "Let me just help you. I had Keegan when I was just eighteen. I'm almost forty-one, she's twenty-two. Hawk and Eagle just turned twenty-eight."

"I would have pegged you for maybe thirty," said Willa, staring at Tinley. "I thought the twins were maybe thirty-five or so. I couldn't figure the math."

"Well, for saying that you're my new best friend," said Tinley. "Believe me, I fought it for a while, but let's just say when Ty… that's Eagle's real name… when he gets his mind set on something, he doesn't give up easily. I couldn't help falling in love with him and now… well, now I have this very large gift coming none too soon."

"Triplets… I can't believe it," said Willa. The women seemed to move closer to Willa, as the men moved around the room discussing the work and no doubt, her brothers. When breakfast was done and the dishes were being cleared, Ghost asked for the team to meet in the conference room, along with Willa. Her heartbeat picked up a few paces, filled suddenly with nerves for no particular reason.

"Come on baby," said Skull, taking her hand. "I'm right beside you the whole time… no matter what." Willa gave him a tentative grin, nodding.

"No matter what."

CHAPTER SEVENTEEN

"Willa, we'd like to back up a bit and get a clearer picture of your family history." Willa nodded at Ghost. "We all know that the three of you were adopted, obviously Craig first."

"No." She shook her head, staring at the table of men.

"No?" asked Ghost.

"No, we were all adopted at the same time. My parents were aid relief workers. They were stationed in Southeast Asia at the time. One day, they were helping to repair the roof of an orphanage, and they noticed Craig sitting on a cinder block in the playground. My dad went down and started chatting with him."

"I don't mean to appear ignorant," said Zulu, "but a black kid in an Asian orphanage?"

"My parents asked exactly that question. The director said he was dropped off when he was just two years old. Obviously, he was very difficult to adopt out being black in an Asian country. The director told my parents that he was very protective of the other children."

"No one could say where his parents were or who they were?" asked Whiskey. Willa shook her head.

"My father started speaking to him and instantly fell in love with him. Craig followed him around all day, and when they would leave in the evenings, he would cry, asking them to return. It didn't take a genius to figure out that they were going to adopt him. When they asked him if he would want to live with them, he said he would, but they had to let his brother and sister come."

"His brother and sister?" asked Ace.

"Yes. Me and Kevin. Kevin was just a little over a year old, and I was a little over three. Craig was already a teenager, way too old to be adopted by most people, but our parents didn't see it that way."

"This orphanage, they had not only a black child, but a clear Caucasian child, and no one questioned it?" said Whiskey.

"I guess not. Honestly, I didn't even think about that until you just said it out loud. It does seem odd that we were all in a place so different from our natural culture. Other than Kevin, of course." She looked at the faces of the men, all without expression.

"Anyway, the adoption was fast. My parents were able to get our papers and passports within just a few weeks. By the time their work was done, they were able to take all three of us home."

"And Craig? Was he always an overprotective brother?" asked Ghost.

"I-I guess so. Definitely with me, at first anyway. I mean, he and Kevin fought on and off. I was so much smaller than both; they didn't really tease me or pick on me. Kevin was hyper-protective of me for some reason. He took all these martial arts classes. Our dad was smart enough to know that he was smaller than everyone else, and it probably made him feel better, safer somehow. When they died, Craig allowed him to continue his lessons."

"You said that Kevin followed Craig around, thought of him as his hero, and that's why he joined the Army. Are you certain of that?" asked Ghost.

"I don't know. I... you're making me doubt everything, to be honest with you. You need to remember when Kevin joined the Army, I was already gone away to college. I wasn't there when he made his decision."

"Did you attend his graduation from boot camp?" asked Zulu.

"I did. He seemed different, but I assumed that was the Army making the change in him."

"Was Craig a dominating brother?" Willa squirmed slightly in her seat, staring at Scott and then the others around the room.

"Dominating?" she whispered. "Wh-what do you mean?"

"Was he abusive at all, Willa? To you, to Kevin, or anyone else."

"N-no, no, he was strict with us. He had to be. I mean, we were pre-teens, and he was this twenty-year-old kid suddenly in charge of us. He had to be strict. He..." Willa's voice trailed off, and she shook her head.

"What was his relationship like with Kevin?" asked Blade. Willa's head snapped up, and she stared into the dark eyes of the long-haired man across from her. Something about his eyes made her feel frightened and cared for all at the same time.

"I knew. If that's what you're trying to ask. I know Kevin is gay. I saw him once after school kissing another guy. They didn't see me, not at first. It was just Kevin and I at home. Craig was still on-base. I swore to Kevin I wouldn't tell anyone, and I never did. Craig never found out."

"He found out," said Blade. "We think he not only found out, but he's using your brother's partner as a pawn in all of this." Ghost looked at Blade with a stern expression. The man had the common sense to nod at his boss.

"Craig. He wouldn't hurt..." Her voice trailed off as she nibbled on her bottom lip, twisting her hands in her lap once again.

"You're not sure, are you?" asked Ace. "It's okay, you know. Sometimes, we don't know for certain whether someone is good at heart or not. It's hard to tell. Your brother provided a home and safety for you, but I'm going to guess that he wasn't exactly the perfect man you've painted him to be."

Willa could feel her eyes filling with tears, the emotions bubbling to the surface in her chest. She shook her head as Skull reached for her hand.

"He-he always had a mean streak in him. He was careful not to show it around our parents, but he would tease mercilessly. I was so much smaller, so much younger. He was careful not to do anything physical with me, but…"

"But what?" growled Skull. Willa stared at him, her eyes filling with tears. "But what, Willa?"

"Skull, brother, take it down a notch," said Gunner softly, staring at his friend.

"Fuck that! You wouldn't take it down a notch if this were Darby. None of you would if it were your woman." The small grins of his teammates made him realize the slip of his tongue.

"Y-your woman?"

"Later," he snapped. "What. What, Willa?"

"As I became a teenager, things changed a little. That's when Kevin became so overprotective. I caught Craig several times watching me get dressed through my bedroom window. I put blinds and drapes up myself to block his view. At first, I thought it was just a mistake, but when it happened a second time, I was scared. I told Kevin, and he told me to make sure I locked the door. He never touched me, never, but he was darned sure looking.

"I'm not sure how he found out about Kevin, but once he did, his teasing was awful. I could hear their arguments. They shared a bathroom, one of those Jack-and-Jill-style bathrooms. I would hear Craig go in while Kevin was changing or showering, and I could hear… I could hear Kevin telling him to leave him alone, to not touch…" Willa bit her lower lip, turning away. Her eyes filled with tears that could no longer be contained.

"When Kevin joined the Army, it seemed to get better. He was off in one location and Craig in another. We were all separate, and that seemed to work better for us. It was Craig's idea to do our weekly calls and keep in touch. Kevin was always quieter, but that was his personality. I mean, I thought it was."

"Willa, we met a man at Fort Bragg who claims he's your brother's partner. Do you know anything about that?" asked Blade.

"No," she said, shaking her head. "Kevin never told me of anyone he dated. I think he always worried that, somehow, I would slip and tell Craig, which I would never do. If he is dating someone, though, I'm happy for him. He deserves to be happy."

"Willa, if you remember, we told you about General Donan claiming that Kevin was a fuckup." She nodded at Ghost. "In our research, we found that Craig was present every time Kevin got into trouble. A few people at a local bar claimed that he started fights with Kevin."

"A bar? Kevin would never go to a bar. He didn't drink. He's a crazy health nut. Doesn't eat red meat, doesn't drink, smoke, or do drugs. He truly treats his body as a temple." Ghost nodded. Blade and Ace doing the same.

"That's exactly what your brother's partner said." Blade continued to stare at the woman.

"I'm sorry, I'm trying to figure out why you think all of this has anything to do with my brothers' disappearance. Were you able to open the file on my laptop?"

"What file?" asked Ace.

"There's a file on her laptop that's password protected. We believe Kevin downloaded it the night they were at her apartment. I forgot to get with you on that," said Ghost, rubbing a big hand over his face.

"No problem, I'll take a look today."

"Is there anywhere your brothers would go? A family vacation home? A friend who would offer them shelter?" Willa shook her head, the tears falling freely now.

"No, no, I don't even know any of their friends. We didn't have any family. It was just us, so I can't think of anywhere. Besides, if Craig is at fault here, wouldn't Kevin be running from him?"

"He might be, honey," said Skull, "but he would be running to somewhere familiar."

"What about the signal of his phone off the coast of Florida?" asked Willa. "Can we go down and investigate that?"

"I can send a couple of guys down," said Ghost.

"No. I want to go. You can send me and... and someone else, but I want to go and try to find my brothers."

"We won't let you risk your life, Willa," said Ghost. "The attack at your home could be a preview of what they're prepared to do. We think your brother, Kevin, gave you something or left something for you that Craig wants. The shipments that are missing at Bragg are weapons, Willa. Not just simple handguns but weapons of war. If Craig is involved, this won't end well for him."

Willa nodded, standing from the table. Each man watched as she circled the room, staring at the photographs on the wall. Some were the crests of every branch of the service. Others were of the finished motorcycles and cars the garage produced.

"I want to be there if you find either one. Please." Skull started to protest, but the slight head shake of Ghost told him he would lose this battle.

"Alright," said Ghost. "I'll send you down there with Skull and Blade. But listen to me, Willa. You will do everything they tell you to do, everything. If you do anything to jeopardize their safety or your own, I will have them hog-tie you and send you back here in a crate. Do I make myself clear?"

Willa swallowed as the big man rose from his seat. She recognized an intimidation tactic when she saw one, and this man was a master at it. Nodding, she approached him with an outstretched hand.

"I promise I won't jeopardize their safety or my own. You have my word." Ghost grinned down at the tiny woman and then at Skull.

"Good fucking luck with this one," he said, shaking her hand. When no one moved, Willa understood and turned toward the door.

"I'll just wait outside for you," she said, staring at Skull. He nodded with a pained expression. She spun on her heel and moved toward him, kissing him softly. "It will be okay. I trust you." They watched as she floated out of the room on a cloud of golden hair, all eyes then turning to Skull.

"Fuck me raw."

CHAPTER EIGHTEEN

Willa noticed that the restaurant was in full swing today. The lunchtime crowd was heavy but not overly so. A couple of young girls were racing around dropping off orders, another girl a bit older, perhaps college-aged, poured drinks at the bar. Spotting a table with Tinley, Grace, and a few other women, she moved slowly toward them.

"Willa! Come join us," yelled Tinley. "Everyone, you remember meeting Willa this morning. Willa, I'm sure you remember Grace. This is my daughter Keegan. Then we have Isabella, she's married to Razor; Taylor is married to Tango; Darby is married to Gunner; Gabi you met the first day as well, she's married to Zulu; Kat is married to Whiskey, but she's at the office today. She's an attorney. You also met Doc that first day. He's married to Bree."

"And finally, our famous author of the group, this is Charlie or better known to most as CC Robat." Tinley smiled, nudging her friend.

"Wait, you're *the* CC Robat?" said Willa, wide-eyed.

"The one and only, but please call me Charlie. I'm married to Ace."

"Oh my God! I've read everything you've ever written! In fact, I used some of what I learned last night on Scott." Her hand flew over her mouth, and Willa blushed a bright red. "Oh shit! Please don't tell him I said that out loud." The women broke out in laughter.

"Honey, we've all used what Charlie has written at some point in our love life," said Grace. "My sex life with Ghost was wonderful, but when I started reading Charlie's books, well, let's just say that's when I got pregnant with Eric."

"Wow! You're the only famous person I've ever met," said Willa innocently.

"I'm not famous, not really. I'm glad you like the books, though, and I'm really glad you like Skull. He's a good one, honey."

"He is," she said, blushing, glancing down at her hands. "He's kind of rough and bristly on the outside, but inside he's really a sweet teddy bear." Grace nodded, smiling at the young woman.

"He's terrific with the kids," said Gabi. "We have twins, Wade and Tyler, both really big babies, and he carries them around, one in each arm like they weigh nothing. He always seems to know when one of us needs a break."

"That's for sure," said Tinley. "When I'm working in the garage, he's checking on me more than Eagle."

"I'll have to change that," said the big baritone voice from behind them. Tinley jumped.

"Damn! Stop doing that! Are you trying to scare these babies out of me?" He kissed her cheek, rubbing her belly in a sweet, tender show of emotion.

"Nope, I'm just checking on my beautiful wife to make sure she doesn't need anything."

"I'm good, honey, really." He kissed her again and disappeared out the side door of the barn.

"That was so sweet," said Willa, grinning at the other woman.

"He's very sweet and attentive. I never thought I'd get married, but when he dug his heels in, I knew I wouldn't be able to fight, and I damn sure don't want to now. That man is amazing in bed!"

"Ewww, Mom! I'm married to his twin!" Keegan playfully wrinkled her nose.

"Normally, Willa, my daughter would be the one without the filter, but since my pregnancy, it seems I just say whatever comes to mind, and I don't give a shit."

"I think you're allowed that when you're carrying three little humans," smiled Willa.

"So, Willa, are you going to be staying with us for a while?" asked Bree.

"You know," said Darby, "for a therapist, you're not very subtle. What my beautiful red-headed friend is trying to ask is are you falling as hard for Skull as he is for you?"

"Oh, I, ummm..." Willa looked up to see several pairs of eyes boring into her. "Listen, I like Scott a lot, more than a lot. From the moment I saw him in that garage, I knew I was attracted to him, and last night proved to me that we are very, very compatible. He's just a little insecure sometimes. It's weird. I mean, women are the ones who are supposed to have insecurities, not men."

"Who told you that bullshit?" said Gabi. Willa shrugged, staring at the gorgeous woman across from her. "Listen, Willa, men are far more insecure than women. We voice our insecurities openly and are usually uplifted by the women around us. The women we consider our sisters, our lifelines. That's what all of these women are to me."

"Amen," said Grace.

"Men don't talk about their insecurities. They don't sit in that conference room and discuss whether their asses are too big, or their dicks too small, or anything else. The guys all know that Skull feels self-conscious of the scar and never talk about it. We, all of us women, we mention it to him. We try to assure him that it's not as bad as he thinks it is. I think a woman rejected him at some point because of it."

"That's the truth," said the big voice walking toward them. George smiled at the women, setting a plate of cookies in front of them.

"What do you mean, George?" asked Willa as she reached for a cookie.

"Skull had only been here a few months when it happened. The bar just opened, and women were flockin' here thinkin' this was some sort of gang or hard-core biker club. It wasn't what the boys wanted, and they made sure to change that perception quick. Skull, he always had that full beard. One night, he came in all shaved and sat at the bar. This woman was talkin' to him, sittin' on the side of him without the scar. He was his quiet, sullen self when she wiggled her way between his thighs, shaking herself against him."

Willa felt herself go stiff, her fists clenching, and then she reminded herself that this was years ago. Besides, she and Scott had not made a formal commitment to one another.

"Skull, he turns, and she sees the scar. Let's just say she was nothin' compared to all you fine ladies. She made a few nasty comments about his face and then said she'd give him a..." George cleared his throat, "... s'cuse the language ladies, a mercy fuck. He just stood all polite like and said thanks, but no thanks. Stayed away for a week before the beard grew back. Some women just ain't right in the head."

"That's awful," said Willa. "Does the woman still come around? I'd like to kick her ass." George chuckled at the thought of the little spitfire in front of him going at it with the woman he remembered.

"No, girl, she ain't been 'round here in years. Don't 'spect she will be either. Blade set her straight. See, she was stupid enough to walk right up to another brother and offer herself. Blade, well, let's just say he don't hold punches with man or woman. She walked out cryin', and he didn't feel one bit of remorse over it."

"I like him more and more," said Willa, straightening her spine. George nodded, laughing at the little woman.

"You ladies enjoy the cookies," he said, nodding at the table.

"So, what will it be, Willa?" asked Bree. "Will you be sticking around for Skull? Are you brave enough to see what happens when this is all done?" Willa looked from one face to the next, each one beautiful in a different way. All these strong, intelligent, gorgeous women surrounding her with love

and advice. Even if Scott weren't here, she would want to be friends with these women.

"Damn right, I will be."

CHAPTER NINETEEN

"Gunner? You think your brother might let us use one of his charters?" asked Skull.

"I'm sure he'd be happy to take you out. I don't think he'd let you run off with his boat, but I know he'll help you out if you need it. I'll give him a call," said Gunner, standing to use his phone.

"What do you think you're gonna find?" said Blade. "She said the ping was right in the middle of the water, several miles off-shore."

"Actually," said Ace, "there are probably a dozen uncharted islands off the southern tip of Florida. The cruise and travel industry found several shallow areas, some that already had sandbars, and built man-made islands for the cruise industry. They drop passengers off on their 'private island' experience for the day and then return them to the ship. They're not really islands at all, but man-made bodies of land they created in most cases, built bars and restaurants, planted trees, it's really clever."

"Wouldn't someone know if they were on one of them then?" said Blade.

"If they're still operational, yes. When the recession hit, many of them were left, and nothing was built on them. I'm trying to gather a map of them now. So far, I have a list of sixteen, and ten are still operational."

"Ten! That makes at least six to search!" said Skull. "That could take us a week."

"No, they're all really small islands. You could walk around them in an hour." Skull nodded thoughtfully.

"If Craig took his brother, maybe he has him on one of those islands," Skull said, looking at Ghost.

"Maybe, but it still doesn't tell us what the hell they're feuding over and what the fuck they want with Willa. Why trash her apartment?"

"Maybe Craig thought she would call him, but he got distracted by the brother," said Blade.

"That's a good thought," said Skull. "If he trashed the apartment, she would get scared and call him. But if Kevin knew something, maybe he distracted him away from Willa."

"It doesn't make sense," said Ace. "Kevin went AWOL long before the apartment was trashed." Skull cursed under his breath, gliding his big hand through his hair and letting his fingers run along the ridge of his scar. Whiskey looked at Ghost and then around the room at the other men.

"She doesn't give a fuck, brother," said Whiskey. Skull's head popped up, his fingers stilling over the scar, his hand quickly falling to the table. "You need to get that shit out of your head. She's crazy for you, Skull. We can see that. She doesn't give a fuck about a scar, and it has nothing to do with her brothers either."

"But she will care. One day she will," he said in a whisper.

"Fuck that!" growled Zulu. "She doesn't care now, and she won't care. She cares about you, brother. That's it."

"We all have scars, Skull. Every last ugly motherfucker of us. Some of them are big and visible, others hidden and eating us from the inside out. Don't let that scar eat away at you, brother. You fought some asshole drug dealer and won. That's a badge of honor. I'm proud to serve with you and call you brother," said Blade, standing. He slapped a hand on his shoulder, nodding. "I'm gonna go pack a bag and gas up the SUV. It'll be better if we don't alert them to any plane tickets." Skull nodded.

"Blade? Thanks, brother." Blade flipped him the finger and walked out, hearing the chuckles behind him.

"He's right, you know," said Whiskey. "She doesn't give a damn about the scar. You need to let that shit go, brother. See what's right in front of you."

"I know. I know, really. Listen, Willa's amazing, but right now, I need to focus on keeping her safe and finding her brothers. Or at least one of them." The others all nodded in his direction, and then Ghost turned to Skull.

"Alright, let's get this shit done. Skull? Check in with us every two hours. Let us know what's happening. Don't forget to wear the watch. You know Ace can track you guys if you're wearing that, and the GPS is turned on as it always should be." He glared at each of the men, intentionally making a dig at them since they often turned their GPS off.

"Got it." Skull started to leave and heard Ghost from behind him.

"Skull? You call me if you need something. Understand?" He grinned at the older man. Although Ghost was only about seven years older, he acted twenty years older sometimes.

"Yes, Dad."

"Fuck you."

CHAPTER TWENTY

"Are you sure you searched her apartment?" he asked the men sitting across from him at the bar.

"We're not fucking idiots, Ross. Yes, we searched the apartment. Ripped everything apart just like you told us to. All those firing pins, the detonators, all that shit would take up a lot of space. There was nothing in her place, nothing."

"Fuck! I don't want to kill this little asshole, but I will if I have to. I'm gonna give him a few more days of starving to death and give him one more chance. In the meantime, enjoy some beach time, pick up a few women, and have some fun. Just don't get caught by the cops for anything. I don't need that kind of heat on me." Both men looked at each other and grinned.

"You want us to pick up a few women and bring them back to the hotel? Have some fun together?"

"Maybe," he said, smiling. "Let me think about it. If I want a woman, I'll find one. Never had a problem getting one on my own before."

"Know that's right," said his friend. "Remember that hot-ass babe you had in Richmond a few weeks ago? Fuck she was hot! Girl had tits so big, you could use them as flotation devices. Was her pussy as hot as it looked?" Craig smiled at his friends, nodding.

"Hotter," he said, taking a swig of his beer. "She took my big black dick and begged for more. I think I kept her a few days before I sold her. She made me some good money, that one. Her tits alone were worth a few grand, but they paid big for her."

"Hey, man," said the man across the table, "I'm all about making money, but these guys are kind of sick, don't you think? I mean, they live in some sort of compound with five or six wives each, popping out kids like candy. When the women can't produce anymore, they just toss them aside or kill them. They don't even get to see their kids again. These women, man, these women could be your sister."

"Exactly," smiled Craig. "I've been trying to grab Willa for years, but you'd be surprised how hard it is to get to her even though she lives alone. I just never had her in the right area at the right time. If I can get her alone, you can be damned sure I'll get a good penny for her, even though she's older than they like."

"How did you even get mixed up with the ROL?" The Ribbon of Life Church and Sanctuary wasn't known to many, and he was careful not to mention their full name in public.

"Met a guy while out one night, and he was trying to recruit me into the church. Told him it wasn't my thing but that I might have a business opportunity for him. That was all she wrote. I've been fucking and drugging women for fifteen years for this guy. Then when they asked for weapons, well, let's just say my bank account grew to a sizeable sum."

He didn't tell them that the rift between he and Kevin started when a fellow soldier Kevin served with disappeared. Kevin was on the search and rescue team, and everything led straight to Craig's door. He knew his brother was lying about having known the woman and found the evidence through a neighbor's video doorbell system. The young soldier was all dressed up for a night on the town when his brother carried her through his apartment door.

Fortunately, Craig realized his mistake and disabled the doorbell before he delivered the girl to the ROL. Kevin hounded his brother with questions, none of which got answered, but that was the beginning of the end of their relationship. Kevin wouldn't let up after that, following Craig nearly everywhere he went.

Craig contacted command and made sure his brother was placed on nights only, citing some family issues that needed to be addressed. When Craig realized that Kevin wasn't going to let things go, he started using the threats against Willa and Adam to get what he wanted and needed. Even drugged the little asshole several times to make sure the shipments were diverted. And since he was the golden boy for General Donan, his idiot little brother was the perfect scapegoat.

The sounds of clinking bottles jolted him to the present, his two men laughing across the table from him. A group of women at a table nearby stood and sauntered their way, the tight skirts and halter tops exposing their glowing tanned skin.

"Fucking love Florida," said Craig. "Let the games begin, boys."

CHAPTER TWENTY-ONE

Skull drove for the first few hundred miles, Willa curled up in the backseat sleeping most of the way with Blade in the front seat. The two men spoke in what Willa assumed was some sort of grunt, man-speak. Their sentences were never more than a few words, and their responses were typically one word, a nod, a laugh, or a grunt; sometimes loud, sometimes soft. She didn't understand it, but then again, she didn't need to.

The long brown hair of Skull brushed the back of his collar, and Willa desperately wanted to reach out and brush it aside, kissing her way around his neck, but common sense prevailed, and she knew that Skull would be embarrassed by her outward show of affection.

Last night, she'd been able to get a better view of his tattoos, most of them on his upper body. An enormous dragon snaked around his arm, curving elegantly over his shoulder and then finally landing, open-mouthed at the back of his neck. The symbol for the Coast Guard was over his left pectoral, and a massive oak tree covered his right side.

There were at least a dozen more, all, she learned, designed by him. His artistic abilities seemed to know no bounds, and it was such a contradiction to the man seated in front of her, she could only shake her head.

"Why are we stopping?" she asked as the vehicle came to a halt.

"Need gas and something to eat," said Blade. She nodded and stretched in the backseat, her back cracked as she did. Stepping from the back of the SUV, Skull noticed how young she looked today. Wearing modestly cut white shorts with a tank top that said *Math is Cool* and several math symbols, he couldn't figure out if he tried. She looked sixteen. Her long blonde hair was pulled back in a ponytail, her face devoid of makeup.

"Are we just grabbing snacks?" she asked Skull.

"We can, but this place actually makes sandwiches and burgers to go. We'll stock up and then hit the road again. You can have the front seat for a while. Blade is gonna drive, and I'll sleep. We want to drive straight through if we can."

"All the way to Miami!?"

"We're stopping just north of Miami, but yes, technically all the way to Miami," said Skull, pulling her into his side, kissing the top of her head. Blade looked down as he pumped the gas, trying not to stare at his friend and his woman. He knew how sensitive Skull was about any relationship with a woman, but he also knew that this one was something special to his friend.

Willa wound her arms around Skull's waist and buried her face in his chest, inhaling the scent she now craved.

"Skull? I wanted to say... last night... last night was the best night of my life. It was perfect, in fact. Thank you," she smiled. Skull nearly fell to his knees. When she began speaking, he was certain she would say that last night was a mistake, but instead, she's claiming it was the best night of her life. Maybe the guys were right.

"Same here, Willa. I'm crazy about you, honey, and I hope we have a lot of 'best nights of our lives' going forward. At least, that's what I'm planning," he murmured against her hair.

"Me too, Skull, me too."

"Come on, you two lovebirds. Let's get some food," grinned Blade.

Skull was right about the gas station; the smell of burgers and greasy fries filled the air, and Willa's stomach rumbled as if on cue. They filled two bags with snacks, waters, and sports drinks, and then ordered food to go. Waiting on the food, Willa felt the vibration of her phone. Looking down, she immediately recognized the number for her brother, Craig.

"What do I do?" she said, panicked, looking up at Skull and Blade.

"Don't answer it, not right now," said Blade. "He'll try to reach you again, but we want to make sure we have a chance to search the area where we know they were last seen first. Is the GPS and locator turned off?" Willa nodded, biting her lower lip. It was killing her to not answer the phone, but she waited patiently, thinking he would leave her a message. When he didn't, her face filled with concern.

"Does he usually leave a message?" asked Skull.

"Always," she said. "Sometimes just 'it's me,' other times it was long, but always. What do you think that means?"

"I think it means we might be right about Craig," said Blade. Willa nodded, walking towards the car. Blade looked at Skull and finally spoke. "She's struggling with this, brother. On one hand, she knows that Craig isn't a good guy, but on the other hand, she can't forget what he did for her and Kevin. We have to make sure she doesn't take his calls until we're ready."

"I know, but it's going to be hard. I can't take her phone away from her."

"Can't you?" grinned Blade.

"Well," smiled Skull, "I can, but I won't do that, not yet anyway. Let's go. We need to put some miles behind us."

It took Skull nearly thirty minutes before he was finally comfortable enough, semi-spread out in the backseat, to close his eyes and catch some sleep. Willa said nothing, staring out the window, eating her burger and fries. Blade would look in her direction every now and then but said nothing as well.

He wondered about the tiny woman in the seat beside him and her true feelings for Skull. It wasn't like him to pry into this brothers' relationships, but Skull was different for all of them.

"So, you and Skull?" he asked. Willa turned toward the stoic man beside her and just stared. He was ridiculously handsome in a rugged, bad-boy kind of way. His long dark waves hitting below his shoulders, rich chocolate eyes, and that perfect five-o-clock shadow, even though it wasn't even three yet. A million women would want this man, but there was something about him that said he was untouchable and, more than that, untamable.

"Yes, at least I'm hoping it will be Skull and me. I really like him a lot. I know we're different, not just physically, but he comes from this normal, middle-American family and home. I'm an adopted nobody who apparently has at least one brother that may be a criminal, possibly two. I know nothing of motorcycles. I can't draw a picture to save my life. I'm so short I need help doing almost everything, and I typically shop for my clothes in the juniors section."

"That's a lot of self-deprecations shoved into one statement," said Blade, glaring sideways at the woman. He glanced briefly into the backseat and saw Skull raise an eyebrow, one eye open. He said nothing, but Blade knew he was listening.

"I know, I'm sorry. It's funny. I said almost the same thing to him about making self-deprecating comments. I just don't understand why he would want me. I mean, he must have women falling all over him at the bar, right?"

"Wrong," said Blade. "First of all, Skull doesn't spend a lot of time at the bar unless it's with all of us. Secondly, he's not a guy that just fucks around. He's particular about the women he spends time with, and I'm being generous by saying 'time.' Listen, Willa, you already figured out that he's pretty sensitive about the scar on his face. Dude took on one of the most feared men in all Southeast Asia and came out on top, just with that little souvenir. He's saved my ass more than once, and if you haven't seen him swim, it's fucking amazing. He's like some sort of overgrown dolphin or something. The truth

is, Skull is a fucking awesome man and brother."

"I know that," she whispered. "It's not him I'm worried about. What if... what if I'm not enough,

Blade? What if he wakes up one day and thinks, 'what the hell am I with this child for'? He could be

with a woman who is tall and voluptuous, someone like Bree or Gabi! I mean, those are gorgeous

women!"

"Yep, they are, but they're not you. He chose you, Willa. Don't let that slip away because of

your insecurities. He chose you, and you chose him. If you hurt him, I'll be paying you a visit, but if

you're serious about him, well, then, I'll be the first one to congratulate you both." Willa smiled at him

and turned slightly to see Skull's sleeping face, although she thought she saw a slight grin on his face as

well.

"Thank you, Blade," she smiled. "Now, what about you?"

CHAPTER TWENTY-TWO

"What about you?" she repeated.

"What about me?" Blade deflected.

"Fair is fair, Blade. You've asked about me, and you know more about me than I know of any of you, so tell me about you. Were you in the Coast Guard?"

"Uh, no. Nothing wrong with being a coasty. It just isn't my thing. I was a Green Beret."

"A Green Beret? Like John Wayne and all that?" Blade chuckled, nodding slightly.

"Yea, I suppose he was the best representation of who we are in movies. We're basically the Special Forces for the Army. We focus on nine different areas of specialty and expertise."

"Wait, were you guys the team that was featured in that movie about the first wave into Afghanistan? The ones that rode the horses or something?"

"Yea," he chuckled, "that was us. We do all sorts of stuff, though. Counterterrorism, the search for WMDs, and even humanitarian missions. That's how I ended up with the Steel Patriots." He said nothing more as Willa patiently waited for him to continue the story, but much like Skull, she was going to have to pry the information from him.

"And?"

"And what?" he grinned.

"And how did that lead you to the Steel Patriots? I swear to God, you two are harder to get information out of than Mata Hari." Blade found himself genuinely laughing, smiling at the little pixie next to him.

"I was working in Honduras helping with cleanup after a hurricane. We were trying to repair buildings, distribute food, administer medical aid, and doing search and rescue. We were overwhelmed, and the Hondurans weren't much help. This was early in the Steel Patriots existence, and Ghost could be convinced to help out just about anywhere back then."

"Not now?" she asked innocently.

"No, now, he likes to stick close to home. We all do. Anyway, Ghost somehow got word that the neighboring Central American and South American drug lords saw this as a prime opportunity to come and kidnap women and children to sell. Him and the team were down there when my team and I found ourselves in a bit of a disagreement with a human trafficker."

"Disagreement?" snorted Willa. "I bet."

"It was getting a little out of hand. I only had five men, and they had more than a hundred when Ghost and the team walked in. It was him, Whiskey, Zulu, Gunner, Tango, Razor, Doc, and Skull. Just Zulu alone would have made them all back off and shit their pants, but when Skull and Zulu walked in, they pretty much realized their shit was cooked."

"That can't be the end of the story," Willa said.

"No, it's not, but it's all the story you'll get. We all had a few beers later that night, and Ghost invited me to join the team. I was coming up on retirement anyway."

"Retirement?" she gasped. "You can't be any older than Skull."

"I'm a couple years older than him. The life of a Special Forces soldier is short, Willa. Literally and figuratively. Normally, we don't last more than ten or fifteen years. We're placed in the most dangerous situations in the world, exposed to ten times the danger the average soldier is exposed to. The beatings on our bodies are brutal. Halo jumps, diving, explosives, it adds up, believe me."

"Well, thank you for all you've done for our country, Blade. Which reminds me, what's your real name?"

"Benjamin. Benjamin LeBlanc. My family is from Lafayette, Louisiana."

"I don't hear an accent. Don't most people from that area have thick Cajun accents?" That brought a laugh to Blade's lips.

"I suppose we do, and I can certainly turn it on if you need me to. I think I forced myself to lose it so I would fit in better with my team. Most of them were from the Midwest or California. They didn't really have any accent at all. I felt like mine was making me sound like some backwoods hick." Willa eyed the man carefully and felt as though there was a backstory there but didn't pry.

"What about a girlfriend? Wife?" And there it was. He'd been waiting for that question and waiting for her to attempt a fix-up for him with some poor, unsuspecting girlfriend.

"Don't have one. Don't want one."

"Okay." Blade turned, giving her a tight gaze.

"Okay?" he said.

"Yea, okay. I respect that. I don't think people have to have a partner to make them feel complete or fulfilled. I think everyone is different. Plus, I think when you find the one, you'll know it. You won't even be looking for her. You'll open a door or something. You'll just trip over her, and there she'll be… or he'll be."

"Definitely a she," he said, grinning. "Not that I have anything against your brother and his preference for men. To each his own. I don't judge."

"So, you've never had anyone serious in your life?"

"I didn't say that," he murmured. Once again, Willa was struck by the seriousness of his expression. It was filled with pain and regret. Things she wasn't willing to dig at. "You should try and get some sleep; it's going to be a long night."

Willa nodded, rolling up her sweatshirt and laying her head against the side of the door. It was only a few minutes, and she was sound asleep. Blade looked in the rearview mirror and knew Skull was awake.

"I know you're not sleeping, asshole," he said in a hushed voice.

"How can I sleep when you girls want to have your slumber party," he grinned.

"Don't be a dick. I was just talking to her."

"I know, man, I was just teasing. I'm sorry she was prying," said Skull, straightening in the backseat. Blade was an extremely private man, and only a few of the teammates knew his full story. As someone who preferred to keep his private life private, Skull could respect that.

"No worries, man. I'll pull over, and you can put the princess in the backseat and sit up here. If you're awake, you might as well be comfortable."

CHAPTER TWENTY-THREE

Ghost propped his feet up on the coffee table, the television on some mindless drivel that he wasn't paying any attention to. Instead, he was following the GPS tracking devices in Blade and Skull's watches. They had just passed the state line of Florida and were on their way to Miami.

He knew that both men were more than equipped and prepared for whatever came their way, but there was also something about this entire thing that made him uncomfortable. It wasn't just the fact that Craig Ross appeared to be jacking with his brother's Army career or that he had some sort of perverted, twisted fascination with his sister. It was more than that.

Grace took the seat beside him on the sofa, curling her legs beneath her. She let one hand slide down the back of his neck, her fingers softly kneading the tense muscles at his shoulders. Ghost closed the laptop, simultaneously closing his eyes.

"You okay, honey?" she asked sweetly.

"Perfect. The boys asleep?" he asked.

"They are both sound asleep. This will be night seven of all-night sleep if they both cooperate."

"Thank you."

"For what? Sleep?" she giggled. He grinned but pulled her onto his lap, her legs on either side of him, straddling his thighs as she nuzzled against his warm neck.

"No. For this. All of this. You, the boys, the house. It's all you, Grace. I wouldn't be half the man I am without you in my life. I thank God every day for you being here. I hate the way it happened, but I damned sure won't question it. I love you, Gracie, so much." He kissed her passionately, his tongue diving between her soft lips. One hand slipped beneath her pajama top, his fingers gripping the full, soft flesh of her breast.

"Oh, Ghost, I love you so much, honey. Please, it's been too long," she cooed. Just as he was about to toss her top to the floor, the doorbell rang.

"Fuck! This better be fucking good," he growled as Grace giggled. "Don't laugh at me, woman. I'm dying of blue balls here!" He pulled the door open to be face to face with a smiling Ace.

"Sorry, Ghost," he grinned. "Hi, Gracie, sorry for the interruption, but I thought you'd want to see this."

"It better be damn good, Ace, or I'm going to tan your hide."

"You can try, old man," he smiled.

"You know, Charlie has certainly made your confidence soar," he snarled. Then he grinned at the younger man, his big arm sweeping towards the sofa. "What do you have?"

"That file on Willa's computer. I finally got into it, and I have to tell you, it wasn't easy. That thing had a ton of protection on it, and not just your average type of protection."

"Okay, so what did you find?" Grace took the seat on the other side of Ace, staring at the computer as well.

"Well, that's just it. I'm not sure. Willa needs to look at this and tell me if she sees anything familiar. I mean, from what I can tell, it's just a collection of photos."

"What do you mean?" asked Ghost.

"Look," said Ace, turning the laptop toward his boss. "See for yourself. They're numbered, so obviously, Kevin wanted her to follow the photos in order. But they don't make any sense at all. It's a photo of a suitcase, then a picture of a crockpot. I mean, a crockpot? What the hell does that mean? The next is a picture of a bookshelf, then it's a photo of what appears to be an attic or maybe a basement. I can't really tell."

CHAPTER TWENTY-SIX

Striker Michaels looked just like his brother, Gunner. He was thick with muscle, dark blonde hair, and brown eyes. All three of the Michaels' brothers looked alike. Hunter was the youngest, living on the West Coast, Gunner in the middle, and Striker the oldest. He'd started with one large charter boat a few years back and now had a fleet that was consistently booked with tourists and deep-sea fisherman alike.

Striker raised his head, his lazy smile reminding them so much of their teammate back home. He waved a hand as he curled the rope on the dock then stepped toward them.

"Hey, fellas! Nice of you to come all the way down here to see me," said Striker.

"Striker," said Skull, pulling him in for a big hug. He slapped his back and released him. Striker faked a cough, gripping his chest.

"Christ! Remember that we're not all super-human, Skull!"

"Don't be an asshole," he growled. Blade pulled him in for a hug as well and grinned. "Striker, this is Willa Ross. Her brother is who we're searching for."

"I'm sorry to hear of your troubles, Willa. The good news is there are quite a few islands in the area your brother's phone last pinged. If he's out there, hun, we'll find him."

"I really appreciate you doing this," said Willa, releasing a breath. "Do we all go together?"

"Actually," said Striker, "I was going to take Blade on this boat and let one of my captains take you two on the charter over there, the *Shellfish*. I'm waiting on him now."

"You know," said Skull, "I did work on the largest cutter in the Coast Guard. I could handle your craft without sinking it." Striker nodded, smiling at the big man, and then looked over his shoulder again, waiting on his captain.

"Yea, yea, I know. Alright, it looks like my guy is gonna be late. Let me just show you a few things on board, and we'll be on our way. I'm sure you know what you're doing, but I just want to be sure you're comfortable. We'll communicate on channel four. I've filed our plan with the Coast Guard, and Gunner knows where we're headed as well. I'm sure he's already filled Ace in."

"What can they do from Virginia?" asked Willa.

"More than you might think, baby," said Skull. "Ace is a genius when it comes to computers, so he could chart our course from a distance, and if we're in trouble for some reason, he could reach out to the police and then the Coast Guard."

"Right," she said, nervously biting her lip. Skull pulled her into his side, leaning against the railing of the boat.

"Do you trust me, Willa?" he asked, kissing the top of her head.

"More than I've ever trusted anyone in my entire life." Willa wrapped her arms tightly around him, letting her head rest against his chest, the beating of his heart thumping against her ear.

"Then trust that I'll make sure you're safe, always." She nodded as Skull walked with Striker inside the wheelhouse. She heard them chatting and then noted the serious tone and lowering voices. She knew they were talking about her and her brothers but didn't feel as though she could tolerate one more discussion about Craig's deception and possibly Kevin's as well.

Feeling the familiar tingling at the back of her neck once more, she turned to scan the docks but found nothing out of the ordinary. Blade walked toward her, smiling.

"Smile big, Tinkerbell," he grinned, "you never know who's watching. We want them to think you're having an enjoyable afternoon with your boyfriend. Business as usual."

"Tinkerbell? Really, Blade?"

"Sorry," he laughed, "but surely you've heard that before."

"I have. Every year I dressed as either a cheerleader, gymnast, or fairy for Halloween. No one would ever believe me as a mean witch or a villain. How would you like it if I called you Master Chief or Aquaman?"

"First of all, I'm impressed as shit that you're making a reference to a video game, bravo! Secondly, I'm also impressed that you're making a reference to DC Comics and making me the star of the show, so hell yea, I'm okay with both of those. Now, how do you know about Master Chief?" he asked.

"Oh, well, a friend of mine from college is a video game designer. He didn't develop that game, but he's done several others."

"Wow, very cool," grinned Blade.

"Hey, you guys ready?" asked Striker.

"Ready as I'll ever be," said Willa.

"Okay then. Blade will come with me, and we'll search these three islands. You and Skull will head to these three. Stay in touch, and let us know if you have any issues. We're going to touch base every thirty minutes. If we don't hear from each other, send out the warning signal."

"Got it," said Willa, looking at the three men. "Let's go find my brother."

CHAPTER TWENTY-SEVEN

Craig watched as the threesome split up between two boats. He briefly thought about splitting up his men but then decided they would need to take out the big man and Willa. He didn't give a shit about the other two.

"Let's go," he said, turning toward the two other men. "We need to get ourselves on that charter without being seen. Wait until the first one is gone, and then climb on from the back deck. Stay below until we know we're clear of the city." The other men nodded in his direction, Matteo quick to follow as usual, but something inside Edgars made him nervous. He couldn't put his finger on it, but he knew this wasn't going to end well for them.

"Got it," said Matteo. The first boat moved quickly out of her berth and toward the open sea. The second revved her engines, moving slowly in a different direction. Willa's blonde head could be seen seated on one of the wheelhouse stools. The big, dark-haired man was towering above her too close for Craig's liking.

The three men made their way below deck, hiding inside the second of the two cabins on board. Craig waited until he knew they were far enough out to sea that it would be unlikely anyone would be near them. Slowly, the three took the steps up, careful to not make any noise, although it wouldn't matter with the huge rumbling of the engines of the big charter.

Willa felt the hairs on the back of her neck stand up and turned, gasping at the sight of her brother and the two other men.

"Hello, baby sister," said Craig. Skull turned quickly, ready to lash out but not before Matteo fired a bullet into his shoulder.

"No!" cried Willa as his body slumped against the wheel. "Don't! Please, Craig, I'm begging you!"

"Begging me? Well, well, well, little sister finally wants to beg me for something. Now isn't this a predicament, but let me ask you, baby sister, what has you in the middle of the ocean so far from home. What the fuck are you doing out here, Willa?" Craig waited as patiently as he could, frustrated that he was even having this conversation with Willa. It wasn't like her to be so curious and brave; he couldn't help but believe the behemoth standing next to her was lending to some of that.

"I'm looking for you and Kevin. That's what I'm doing. What's going on, Craig? What are you doing? My apartment was completely trashed. Everything was destroyed. Did you do that?" she asked with tears in her eyes.

"Me? No, I would never do that," he smiled, feigning innocence. "Matteo and Edgars did it." The other two men laughed as Skull stood, blood oozing from the shoulder wound. Suddenly, the smiles were gone from their faces. He acted as if it were nothing more than a mosquito bite, his big body standing tall and erect, protectively shielding Willa.

"I guess one bullet won't do," said Matteo, lifting his weapon again.

"No!" cried Willa. Craig held up his hand and smiled at his sister.

"You want the big man to go free? Fine, tell me where it is?" he sneered.

"Where what is?" asked Willa, exasperated.

"You know exactly what I mean. You and Kevin were alone when I went to get the pizza. I know he gave it to you. Where did you put everything?" asked Craig.

"I have no clue what you're talking about," cried Willa, clinging to Skull's big body. "Kevin didn't give me anything! You two were late and didn't even stay a full three hours, for goodness' sake! I have nothing of his or yours. Where is Kevin? What have you done, Craig?"

"Kevin? Oh, you mean our sweet little fairy brother. The one who likes dicks more than pussies?" The disdain in his voice made Willa wince. When had the hate creeped into him so deeply? Was it there their entire lives, or did something happen to make it come out?

"Don't be crude, Craig. None of that matters. This is Kevin, our brother!"

"He's not my brother," said Craig. Skull couldn't stand it any longer. He stood silently, letting Willa ask her questions, but now he knew; he knew that Craig was the problem here, and whatever was happening, it really didn't matter. He needed to keep Willa safe and find Kevin if he was still alive.

"You're a pathetic excuse for a soldier," said Skull. "You're a disgrace to the uniform and the brotherhood." Craig's face flamed with embarrassment, Matteo and Edgars took a step back; the quick temper of their boss was not something they wanted to be in the line of.

"Don't you fucking judge me, you hippy reject!" Willa stepped forward, bravely facing her brother in Skull's defense.

"Hippy? He's not..." Skull gripped her shoulder, squeezing to let her know he didn't want to give them any information about him that they might use.

"It's okay, Willa. He can call me whatever he wants. It won't change what he is. I know enough that the Army's calling is to protect others, not harm them. I know that somehow, you've fooled your commanding officers or manipulated them to believe what you want."

"Shut your fucking mouth!" yelled Craig. "You know nothing! I worked for twenty years to support the two of them, give them everything they ever wanted. Dance lessons, gymnastics, cheerleading. Do you know how much that shit costs? Did you honestly believe I could afford all that on my salary? Then all the karate and tai kwon do for the little fruit fly."

"Stop calling him that!" yelled Willa. "He's a good, kind, decent man, and he is a damned good brother. I would have given you anything, Craig. All you had to do was ask. I made millions selling my software. You knew that. If you needed money, why didn't you just ask?" Craig laughed at her.

"First off, I will have all your money once you are dead. Remember? I'm the executor of your will and beneficiary, along with our brother Kevin of course. Speaking of which, he *was* our brother. *Was*. He was a damn good brother, I suppose, as brothers go anyway. Now, you two are going to meet his fate." Skull saw his chance to take him, but he didn't see Matteo coming from his blind side, the butt of the pistol slamming against his head. His big body crashed to the floor, slumping against the shining deck, Willa at his side.

"Throw them overboard. If they're lucky, they'll swim to Kevin, a sort of three for one funeral," he sneered. Willa cried over Skull's body, his head bleeding profusely, his shoulder still dripping thick crimson slowly through his shirt.

"What happened to you? When did you change?" she cried, staring up at her brother.

"I've always been this way, little Willa. You just didn't see it. I hated you and Kevin from day one. Both so perfect and cute, everyone was looking to adopt the two of you. I spent ten years in that fucking hell hole of an orphanage. Ten years being the only black kid in an orphanage in Asia. No one could figure out how I ended up there, and no one cared. I became their errand boy, the one responsible for the rest of you brats. When the Ross's showed up, I figured if I could convince Mom and Dad that we were all together. We'd be adopted together."

"What have you done, Craig? Why are you doing this? I deserve to know why you killed my brother and are going to throw me to the sharks!"

"Money, baby sister. It's all about the money. I gave everything to the two of you, and now, I'll have everything. I was given an opportunity, and thanks to Kevin making it easy for me, I was able to formulate an unbreakable plan. Of course, Kevin had to go and fuck it up for me. No matter. I plan on retiring someplace warm and inviting, all the women catering to my needs."

Willa shook her head, her cool fingertips tracing the gash at the side of Skull's head. Tears streamed down her face, then remembering what Striker said, she knew that if they could survive for at least a little while, when they didn't check in, he would send out the army for them. Or the Coast Guard or someone.

Matteo and Edgars tried to lift Skull, groaning under the enormity of his weight and size. Skull damn sure wasn't going to make it easy for them. He pretended to be dead weight as much as possible but also didn't want to be injured further.

"Fuck, he's a big piece of shit," groaned Matteo.

"Shut the fuck up!" screamed Craig. "Just toss his big ass overboard." Willa tried to free herself of her brother's grip, but he held firm as she watched Skull hit the water.

"Scott!" she yelled.

"Scott? Isn't that cute? You know, I was going to toss you with him, but maybe I'll keep you for myself." He leered down at her, that tight, muscular little body calling out to him. They weren't blood-related; it wouldn't matter if he tasted her before selling her off.

Panic bubbled up within Willa as her brother's wild eyes raked up and down her body. Remembering what little she'd learned from Kevin about self-defense, she jammed her knee into her brother's crotch and then stepped hard on his instep. The other two men stood frozen, just long enough for her to grip the railing and do a perfect backflip into the water.

Diving for Scott, she felt his collar and pulled, kicking with all her might, surfacing and attempting to grip him around the shoulders and keep both of them afloat.

"You're going to fucking die, Willa! Is that better than being with me?" yelled Craig.

"Anything is better than being with you," she replied, spitting out salt water.

"So be it. Die, bitch, and say hello to Kevin when you get to hell. Let's go," he said, turning to the two men.

"Oh God, oh God, what do I do now?" she cried, desperately trying to tread water with Skull's weight leaning against her. The big engines roared, and she watched as her brother and the two men sailed from sight.

"Scott, Scott, please, please, honey, you can't die. You just can't! I haven't told you that I love you yet. I have to tell you, please, Scott," she cried. She heard Skull moan and looked down into his face.

"Are they gone," he whispered.

"Yea, baby, they're gone. Please stay with me." Skull suddenly swirled in the water, facing her. He gripped her waist, pulling her to him and wrapping her legs around his own and her arms around his neck. He kissed her furiously, tasting her, and then pulled back.

"I'm in love with you too, Willa."

"You... you're okay. You're not dying?" she asked.

"I'm okay. I was trying to make them believe I was out of it. Remember, my name is Skull for a reason, honey. Hard head," he grinned. "Gonna take a lot more than this to break my head open. They said the island Kevin was on isn't far from here. If my calculations are right, it shouldn't be more than a mile in that direction. It was on our list to search."

"A mile!" screeched Willa. "A mile in this water? Scott! We're going to die. There are sharks and jellyfish, and I don't know what else. We can't swim a mile."

"Sure, we can, baby," he smiled, kissing her lips once more. "Just an easy swim, and it's a beautiful day. Crawl on my back and just hold onto my shirt. Grip it lightly, don't choke me or inhibit my arm movement. I'll do all the work."

"You can't swim for both of us!"

"Yea, baby girl, I can," he said, kissing her again. "Don't argue, Willa. We gotta get moving."

Willa did as he asked, gripping the back of his shirt as he checked his watch and then turned slightly in the water. She felt his big legs kick out, his upper body lowering in the water, and then his powerful arms and shoulders propelled them through the vast ocean of blue and green water at a ridiculous pace. Willa knew he would never be able to keep it up, not for a whole mile! His hard thrusts and movements made them glide through the water, and Willa felt as though she knew what it must be like to swim with the dolphins.

Blade was right. Skull was an amazing swimmer, powerful and graceful, despite his size. He stopped once to check his watch, and she asked if he was okay. Only giving her a thumbs up, he turned slightly to the south and began swimming once more. Nearly distracted by the speed at which they were moving, Willa looked up to see the rich green fronds of a small grouping of palm trees, surrounded by lush vegetation and a few scattered, dilapidated buildings. Tapping his shoulder, Skull stopped.

"Look! I think that's it," she cried.

"That's it, baby," he said, barely losing a breath. "Can you swim from here?" Willa nodded, following beside him until they hit the sandy beach, crawling onto the warm sand. Willa's legs were burning from the short swim, but she knew Scott's must have been on fire.

"You okay, baby girl?" he asked.

"Yep, but if you find a volleyball, I'm gonna have a serious meltdown."

CHAPTER TWENTY-EIGHT

"So, how are Gunner and Darby doing?" asked Striker, maneuvering through the calm waters of the Atlantic.

"Good," said Blade, looking sideways at the other man. "Don't you talk to them?"

"Well, yea. I mean, I call him and all, but it's usually these short grunting conversations. If I want to know how things are really going, I have to speak to my beautiful sister-in-law or that precocious niece of mine." Striker laughed, shaking his head at some of the things that came out of sweet little Calla's mouth.

"You should come up and see us," said Blade. "You're always welcome. You know that."

"Yea, I know. The business is doing great now, and we're really starting to get a lot of repeat business. I suppose we could take a bit of a break. It's just that, well, Laura..."

"Let me guess. She doesn't like the whole military biker vibe happening at Steel Patriots."

"You apparently know my wife," he grinned. "I don't know, man. Laura and I used to be on the same page with everything, and then these last few months, it seems like we're not on the same page for anything! I want kids. She used to, and now, suddenly, tells me she wants to wait. We went into this business together, but now she wants to go to work for some law firm."

Blade just nodded, unsure of whether Striker wanted him to voice an opinion or simply to be there as an ear for him. He was put out of his misery as the first island came into view.

"That's it," said Striker, "that's the first one. We'll anchor and swim to shore." Blade nodded, stripping off his t-shirt and shorts, his swim trunks beneath. Striker turned and smiled at him.

"What? You don't like my trunks?" asked Blade, looking down at the bright yellow cartoons on his shorts.

"Minions? Really? What are you, six?"

"Most of the time, I'm seven, but today I'm six. No, asshole, it was all they had at the store. I totally forgot to bring a pair. Let's go."

Striker anchored the big boat, and both men dove off the back toward the island. As they reached the sandy shore, the two men walked along the beach of the tiny island.

"Let's check some of those buildings," said Blade. Reaching behind him, he withdrew the long blade from its scabbard.

"What the fuck is that?!" yelled Striker.

"Protection, dumb ass."

"You had that tied in your swim trunks? Did you expect trouble?" asked Striker.

"No, I expected sharks. Skull might like living in the water, but I prefer most of my H2O contact to be in the shower or in a glass. Let's check this one," he said, pointing the closest building. Blade shoved on the door. The rusted hinges gave way, splintered wood nearly crumbling at his feet. No one had been in this building in ages.

Moving to the next building, they found the same. Two more buildings were on the island, but both were nearly kindling. Nothing showed any signs of occupation.

"He wasn't here," said Blade.

"Definitely looks that way. Let's head back to the boat and see if we can contact Skull and Willa. Are those two serious, by the way?"

"Yea," grinned Blade. "Not sure either has admitted it yet, but they're damn sure serious. He deserves it. I don't know Willa that well yet, but from what I can tell, she's pretty awesome."

"That's good to hear," said Striker, smiling.

As the two men stepped back on the boat, Striker immediately went to the radio.

"*Shellfish*, come in. *Shellfish* come in, over." Striker waited a few minutes and, hearing nothing, started to feel the unease that came with years of experience. "*Shellfish* come in; *Shellfish* come in, over."

"They're not answering. Do you have GPS on the boat?" asked Blade.

"Of course, I do," sneered Striker as he turned to the computer system. "This doesn't make sense. It's docked at the marina."

"Fuck!" Blade grabbed his phone and dialed. "Ace? Where is Skull? Yes, I know we were together, but we split up, and he was on another boat."

"He has GPS on you guys?" asked Striker.

"Yea, in our watches. It helps them keep... yea, send me the coordinates," said Blade. "He's got him. Sounds like he might be on one of the islands we charted. Let's go."

CHAPTER TWENTY-NINE

"What should we do? Build a signal fire?" asked Willa. Skull smiled at her, looking around the island and then across the open water.

"No, not yet, honey. We have plenty of daylight left, and if I know Blade, and I do, he'll figure out what's happened and be here soon. Why don't you and I check around the island and see if we can find anything?" Willa nodded, taking his hand as they walked around the shoreline. Skull stopped, picked up three empty beer bottles, and frowned.

"Do you think that's just from some kids?" she asked.

"I don't know," he said, looking around. "It's pretty far out for teens. It could have been just random boaters using the island as a party stop. Let's just be careful and watch for any other signs."

Willa nodded again, dutifully following him as he moved slowly around the terrain. She thought back to Craig and his statements about her and Kevin. He always seemed fine with raising them, supporting them. He never openly complained to either one of them. If at any time he couldn't afford something, they both would have accepted it. Why all this anger now.

"You okay, baby?" he asked, looking down at her.

"I like when you call me that," she said, wiping away a tear. "Even though you were hurt back there, although I didn't realize you weren't hurt that bad, I've never felt so safe, Scott. My brother was acting crazy. You were shot and injured, and still, I felt completely safe."

"So, you like that you feel safe around me?" he said, pulling his hand away from hers.

"Don't do that," she pleaded, "don't pull away from me now. We've been through too much, Scott. Yes, I love that I feel safe around you, but it's *you*, Scott, you that I love. I know it's only been a few weeks, but I know that you're a good man, kind, generous, decent, sexy." She grinned up at him and took a few quick steps to turn and stand in front of him, placing one hand against his chest.

"Look at me, Scott. I love you. If you were five-foot-seven or seven-foot-five, it wouldn't matter. It's the man you are that I love and want to get to know more." He nodded, kissing her forehead.

"Sorry, baby, it's that ugly monster creeping up."

"I'm not her, Scott," she said. He looked shocked and started to step around her, but Willa wouldn't let him pass. "I'm not the woman who hurt you or any woman other than me. You're not the man who hurt me or any man other than Scott. We are Willa and Scott. That's all, and for me, that's enough. Is it enough for you?"

Scott looked down into those big green eyes, pleading with him for the response she needed but, more importantly, wanted. Her eyes, soulful and yearning, he was lost in their depths. She was right. She wasn't any of the women he knew before. She was Willa, his Willa.

"It's more than enough, baby girl," he said, pulling her body against his. Their passionate kiss felt like a scene from a movie, the water lapping onto the beach, the sun shining down. Remembering their mission, they both separated, smiling.

"Let's check out that building over there. It looks newer than the others," he said. As they walked toward the metal shed, Skull noted the trash littering the worn path and slowed, unease settling at his spine. Willa followed close behind, her hand resting lightly at the top of his shorts.

"Step back," he said, reaching for the door. Flinging the door open, he moved carefully into the dark space, feeling around for the latched window. Opening the window, he turned and nearly gasped out loud. In the center of the building was a small cage, much like a kennel. Inside it was what he assumed was Kevin Ross.

"No! No, no, no! Kevin!" said Willa, kneeling beside the cage. "Kevin, please answer me, please!"

"Baby, I need to see if he's still breathing. Step back." Willa reluctantly moved back as Skull's big hand reached between the narrow bars. He placed two fingers at the bony wrist of Kevin Ross, waiting. "He's alive, barely."

"Oh, God," she cried. "Kevin, please, I'm here now. Please don't die."

"Willa, baby, I need you to see if you can find a freshwater source or bottles of water. If Craig and the other two assholes were coming out here, they might have left a few supplies. Check the other buildings, okay? Willa?"

"No, no, I can't leave him. I can't..." Skull nodded.

"Okay, honey. You stay with him. Keep talking to him while I search." Willa immediately knelt beside her brother, taking his hand in her own, now almost the same size. Skull propped the door open to let fresh air filter into the warm shed, then opened the other window as well. Light peppered the space, giving them the first full view of Kevin's body, the sight of it made Willa gasp at the emaciated frame of her brother.

Skull took off in a jog, darting between the half dozen sheds on the island. His hunch was right. Craig and the others left a half case of bottled water, some beef jerky, a few oranges, and two sports drinks. It was exactly what Kevin needed right now.

Filling his arms with as much as he could carry, he made his way back towards Willa and Kevin. He stopped in his tracks, raising his head at the familiar sounds. Hearing the loud roar of engines, he ran toward the shed, handing the things off to Willa.

"Stay here! Do not move, no matter what you hear. Give him water first, and then try to get him to eat that orange."

"Where are you going?" she asked, panicked. "Don't leave me! Please, Scott!" Skull leaned down beside her, brushing back the long stray blonde strands from her face.

"I would never leave you, honey. Someone is coming. I just want to make sure it's the good guys." She nodded as he kissed her lips, then turned her attention to her brother.

Skull took off toward the beach, following the shoreline around toward the sounds of the engines. Just as he reached the area for a clear view, he spotted Blade slicing through the water. As he helped him ashore, he pulled him in for a brotherly hug.

"Fucking glad to see you, brother," he smiled.

"What the fuck? You're bleeding!" He waved a signal to Striker, indicating they would need medical support. Skull watched and then told him the news.

"We're gonna need a chopper to get Kevin off the island. He's alive, barely."

"There's nowhere to land here, brother. Let's get the Coast Guard out here, and they can speed up the process." Skull nodded again as Blade motioned to Striker.

"Let's go."

CHAPTER THIRTY

Willa lay on the sand-covered floor, her hand gripping Kevin's. She'd been able to get a little bit of water into him, but he refused to open his mouth for the orange. His body was littered with bruises and cuts, his eyes swollen shut.

"You have to stay with me," she sniffled. "Scott, my boyfriend, is getting help. I suppose I should tell you I have a boyfriend. He's wonderful, Kevin. He's kind and strong. He's the sweetest man I've ever met, and I'm truly in love with him."

Kevin said nothing, his chest barely moving with shallow breaths. His once thick, dark hair seemed thinner somehow, and Willa fought back a new wave of tears.

"He's been helping me to find you and Craig," she said. That seemed to bring a reaction from Kevin. Her brother stirred slightly, the failed attempt at opening his eyes not lost on Willa.

"It's okay, Kevin. We know about Craig. You're going to be okay. You have to be," she whispered beside him again. "I love you."

A big shadow cast over the space, and Willa gasped, turning to see Scott and Blade, releasing a big breath, tears streaming down her face in relief.

"It's okay, baby," said Skull, kneeling beside her, "we've got help coming. Blade's going to get the lock off the cage, and then we're going to move him to the beach. I need you to go with Striker and wait for the Coast Guard. Can you do that for me, honey?" Willa nodded, kissing the back of her brother's unrecognizable hand. Standing, she followed Striker toward the beach.

"Holy fuck, he's a mess," said Blade.

"Yea. If I get my hands on Craig, that prick is mine." Blade nodded, looking at Skull once more, seeing the blood that he'd missed on the beach.

"You okay?" he asked.

"This? Yea, bastard shot me in the shoulder and then slammed his pistol against my head. Shoulder hurts like a bitch, but my head is fine." Blade chuckled, focusing on the lock once more. Hearing the click, he grinned and pulled the mechanism free.

"Still got it," he smiled. Gently lifting the shoulders of Kevin Ross, they moved him carefully from the filthy cage to the floor of the hut. Moaning, Skull caught the faint breathless whispers of Willa's name, then Craig's.

"It's okay, brother," said Skull softly. "Willa is safe. I promise I'll keep her safe."

"Cr-craig... kill..."

"Yea, I know. When we find Craig, we'll kill him. No worries there," he snarled. Kevin shook his head listlessly side to side.

"N-no... kill-er... Craig killer..." Blade frowned, looking down at the man, Skull staring at his face.

"Okay, Kevin, we get it. He's a killer. Just rest, brother. We'll get him." The distinct sounds of a Coast Guard cutter and helicopter were heard around the island, and Skull knew that the cavalry had arrived.

As chaos came down around them, the Coast Guard medics took over, starting an IV on Kevin and immediately dressing his most serious wounds. Although Skull pushed back initially, with Willa's prodding, he allowed them to dress his wounds as well.

"You're not Superman, you know," she said with a feisty hand on her hip. As Kevin's body was brought out on the litter, she gasped seeing him in the sunlight, his face almost unrecognizable.

"What's the deal?" asked Skull to the medic.

"Malnourished, dehydrated, looks like he was hit multiple times with a taser or cattle prod. If we can pump him with fluids and get some of the worst cuts taken care of, he'll be okay." Skull nodded as they quickly moved him toward the beach.

The helicopter was able to lift him aboard, whisking him away to the nearest trauma center. Willa, Skull, Blade, and Striker took the charter back and then made their way to the hospital. By the time they arrived, Kevin had been cleaned up, bandaged, and was on a steady flow of fluids and antibiotics, already showing improvement.

"Is he okay?" asked Willa to the attending physician.

"Another day or two, and he wouldn't have been. You got to him in time. He's awake, but I wouldn't count on getting a lot out of him. He just keeps murmuring two words—Craig and killer." Willa nodded, nibbling her lower lip to prevent the tears threatening to spill. Turning from the other men, she entered her brother's room, sitting beside him once again to hold his hand.

"You're going to be okay," she whispered. "I'm going to call Adam and let him know."

Kevin's head turned toward his sister's voice, his eyes widening as much as possible. Was he dreaming, or did she just say she knew about Adam?

"I know, Kevin. I've always known. I love you, and I'm thrilled that you've found someone to love too. I just need you to get better now." Willa turned to hear Skull and Blade enter the room.

"How is he, baby?" asked Skull.

"I don't know," Kevin murmured something low as he turned his head toward Skull's deep voice.

"Hey, man, it's okay. You're going to be okay now. My name is Skull, and this is Blade. We're part of the Steel Patriots, and we're helping your sister. You're safe now." He shook his head, murmuring once again. "What is it, brother?"

"Cr-craig…"

"Yea, we know he was holding you, and he's behind this," said Blade.

"Killer… weapons… stole…" he sucked in a breath, pain racking his body.

"He stole weapons?" questioned Skull. Kevin's head nodded.

"Laptop… folder…"

"The folder on my laptop? Yes, we opened it, but it's just pictures," said Willa. "I don't understand." Kevin took a deep breath and turned toward the table, eyeing the water. Willa dutifully placed the straw between his lips, allowing him to drink as much as he wanted.

"Craig is working with the ROL," he said breathlessly. "Selling weapons, women…"

Blade immediately turned to Skull, nodding as he stepped outside, his phone already dialing Ghost.

"He wants Willa. Can't let him…"

"Not fucking happening, brother," growled Skull. "He won't touch either one of you; I can promise you that."

"What are the pictures of?" asked Willa. "I haven't seen them, but I was told they're just random." Kevin nodded, his eyes fluttering as he did.

"Damn!" said Skull. The doctor entered the room, checked his vitals quickly and the flow of the IV.

"He'll be fine. Once we have him stabilized, we can transfer him to a home hospital."

"We'd like to transfer him to our clinic in Virginia," said Skull. The doctor nodded, asking several questions of Skull about the facilities at the clinic and who would be the attending physician. Finally, deciding it would be easier for him to speak with Gabi and Doc, he gave him the contact information and sent a text, giving the two a heads up.

Skull watched the doctor leave once again, then gripped Willa's shoulder as Blade came back into the room.

"Ghost has been notified. He's contacting Ivan and a few other friends to see what the ROL is. They're getting a place ready for Kevin and bringing Adam up, so he'll be there when we arrive." Skull nodded.

"Doc said as soon as he's stabilized, we can move him. Airlift will be expensive as shit…"

"I'll pay for it," said Willa, her eyes never leaving her brother's face. "Whatever it costs, I'll pay for it. I want my brother home where he belongs with the man he loves." Skull just nodded.

"Okay, baby girl, we'll arrange it."

Blade gave him that look, the one that said everything with just a stare. Now, all they had to do was figure out what the fuck Craig was doing and who the fuck the ROL was.

Walk in the park.

CHAPTER THIRTY-ONE

Skull had to practically pry Willa from her brother's bedside. Finally, able to place two Dade County Sheriff's deputies at his room, ensuring her of her brother's safety, they made their way back to the hotel.

It was almost nine by the time they entered their rooms, exhausted, dirty, and more than a little sun and wind burned. Willa took the shower first, taking her time to rinse the salt water and sand from her body, happy to finally have clean hair. As she wrapped the towel around her small frame, she remembered the sight of her brother's starved body and held back a sudden need to cry. Crying wouldn't help him now, and it would only make Skull more uncomfortable. Brushing her teeth and running a comb through her long hair, she twisted it to the side and stepped from the steam-filled room.

"Feel better?" grinned Skull.

"A little," she smiled. "I'm really hungry. How about you?"

"Way ahead of you, beautiful," he smiled. "I ordered room service for all of us."

"All of us? Hey, wait, you're showered. How did you get showered?" she asked.

"We have adjoining suites with Blade. He stayed in here while I took a shower in his room. He's over there showering now, and then we'll both be out and clean when room service arrives. You won't have to answer the door." Willa gave him a sly grin, her hand resting at her hip.

"So, let me get this straight. You left your friend in this room while I was showering, not knowing whether or not I might come out completely naked to tempt you?" Skull started to speak when Blade walked into the room.

"Never happen, beautiful," he grinned as he opened the adjoining door. "I waited for the water to turn off and was going to yell out that I was in the room. I do not want to risk the wrath of my brother." Willa giggled as the two men smiled. Realizing she was still just standing in a towel, she pulled a pair of soft cotton pajamas from her bag. A bra was completely unnecessary considering the size of her breasts, plus the camisole top had a built-in shelf bra.

Excusing herself to the bathroom once more, she dressed quickly and then braided her wet hair. When she entered the room, the men were waiting at the table, a myriad of delicious dishes on display for their choosing.

"Oh wow! You really did order a selection," she smiled.

"You might want to get yours first, Blade. As you saw earlier, little bit here can almost out-eat me," Skull grinned at her as she reached for the big cheeseburger. Blade wondered if she might get upset by the comment but almost immediately knew she was used to the teasing.

"Ha ha, funny man. I'm not embarrassed that I can eat more than most grown men. I love it. This cheeseburger is just the beginning for me. I'll eat the fries, then start in on the pasta, and for my finale, I think I'll eat the cheesecake." She narrowed her eyes at both men. "You touch any of it, you'll have to deal with me."

Blade laughed, throwing both hands in the air as they dove into the food. He was shocked to see that Skull was right, Willa ate more than most men he knew, and that was saying a lot. He'd watched her inhale their breakfast but honestly believed it was an anomaly. Just as they set the trays into the hallway of the hotel for pick up, Skull's cell phone rang.

"It's Ghost," he said, hitting the speaker button. "Hey, brother, we're all here, and you're on speaker."

"Good. Are you okay, Willa?" His voice was so filled with familial concern, making Willa want to cry, but instead, she nodded her head, grinning at the phone.

"I'm good, Ghost. Thank you for asking. Skull and Blade are taking great care of me, and I owe my brother's life to them."

"That's what we're here for, honey." Skull could almost see the small smile slipping from the lips of his boss. "I heard back from Ivan about the ROL. It's known as the Ribbon of Life Church and Sanctuary. They have a large compound in West Virginia. Basically, the men believe in polygamy, taking as many wives as they can and popping out kids as fast as they can."

"You said the men believe in polygamy," said Willa.

"Smart woman, Skull. You better damn sure keep her." Skull grinned. "Ivan said his contact believes the women are drugged and kidnapped, often broken in or trained by other men first and then sold to the ROL."

"Oh, God," whispered Willa. "You… you're saying that Craig… Craig helped these people."

"I'm afraid so, Willa. It looks like your brother has been helping them for about twenty years. When he finds young women that have no families to care whether they disappear or not, he lures them in, drugs them, enjoys some time with them, and then either trains them for the ROL or simply sells them to the elders, and they decide."

"But polygamy isn't legal in West Virginia," said Willa.

"Technically, honey, it's not legal anywhere," said Skull.

"He's right. There's more, though. Once these women pop out four or five kids and reach a certain age, they're disposed of."

"Disposed of?" asked Willa. Skull and Blade looked at one another, staring down at the phone, waiting for Ghost to respond.

"I'm sorry, Willa," said Ghost. "When they're done with these women, they either kill them or sell them to someone else. Some could be as young as twenty-five when they're finished, depending on how they look. Their life is not easy, so these women age fast."

"What does this have to do with weapons?" asked Blade.

"That's the other issue. Ivan claims that the ROL put out feelers months ago for weapons. It seems they want to create a private army or at least arm the one they have."

"This could be another situation like we saw in Texas a few years back," said Skull.

"It's exactly what they're worried about at the bureau," said Ghost. "Listen, Gabi spoke to the hospital, and Kevin is scheduled to be transferred here in the morning. Why don't you three get on the road early? We'll take care of everything here with Kevin. He'll be all settled in by the time you get home."

"Thank you, Ghost. Thank you for taking care of my family," said Willa.

"You are family, Willa. I have no doubt that big asshole has made it clear that you belong to him now. That makes you family, and definitely by connection, your brother as well. Although you'll have to forgive me for not extending the invite to Craig."

"I understand," she said with a sad grin.

"Alright, get some sleep, and I'll see y'all in a day or so. Check in with me often." Blade and Skull grinned, then spoke in unison.

"Yes, Dad." Willa couldn't help but giggle.

"You're assholes. Fucking assholes." The line went dead as they all chuckled, Willa shaking her head at the brotherly affection.

"I'm headed to bed," she said, standing. "Thank you both for today, for saving my brother." She kissed Blade on the cheek and then turned to Skull, wrapping her arms around his neck and working her legs between his big, thick thighs.

"And you," she said, kissing his lips, "I'll see you in a few minutes, I hope, but thank you, and if you forgot, I love you." Willa kissed him long and hard, his big hands gripping her muscular ass cheeks. When she finally pulled away, Blade was grinning ear to ear at his friend, watching her move into the bedroom.

"Don't say it," said Skull.

"Say what? That you're a lucky bastard, and you'd better not do anything stupid to fuck this up? Is that what you thought I would say?"

"Asshole."

"Yea, but I'm your brother, asshole." Blade laughed, standing to move toward his room. "See you in the morning."

Skull sat for a long time, just thinking, his insecurities creeping up once again. Then, as if Blade slapped him in the back of the head, he stood.

"What the fuck are you doing?" he murmured to himself. "You've got a beautiful woman in there waiting for you." Opening the door to the dark bedroom, he maneuvered to the empty side of the bed. Stripping his clothes off, he lay against the cool sheets, his bare body without cover.

Willa scooted closer to him, her warm hand resting lightly on his abdomen, her leg riding up his thigh. She'd waited for him, hoping he would come in soon, and now here he was, smelling clean and masculine, his big body ready for her. Touching the wound at his shoulder, she leaned forward, kissing it.

Skull smiled at her tenderness. He barely felt the wound, yet her sweet touch made him feel as though he could conquer the world. Letting his arm fall around her body, he was surprised to find she'd removed her pajamas, now completely naked beside him. Rubbing his rough, callused hand up and down her back, he nudged her closer to his hot body, turning to take her mouth in a possessive kiss.

Willa's moans filled his soul as she writhed against him, the wetness of her soft curls dripping against his thigh. Her small hand gripped the rigid mass jutting toward the ceiling, gliding up and then all the way down, gripping his heavy full sacks.

"Fuck, baby girl," he groaned.

"Yea, fuck," she said, kissing him as she sprawled on top of him, straddling his thick thighs. "I need you to fuck me, Scott. Please, honey." She moaned against his lips, rubbing her hard nub back and forth against his stiff cock.

Scott gripped her hips, pushing her against the bed. He lifted both knees, holding them in place curled over his elbows. Her legs spread wide, the sweet pink wetness waiting for him. The tip of his cock touched her opening, and he couldn't look away, watching it stretch her, invade the tiny hole so damp and ready for him.

"Oh fuck, Willa," he growled.

"Yes, yes, Scott, more..." He nodded, sliding in further, feeling her stretch once more for him, her body still so tight and unused to his size and girth. The warmth of her walls closed around him, squeezing him, the heat penetrating his most sensitive skin.

"Oh shit, baby, you're so fucking beautiful, Willa. So hot..." She shook her head, kissing him, pulling him into her small body.

"It's you, Scott. You make me so hot. I need you. Please, baby, I'm so close..." He could only nod, drilling into her faster with more purpose. He felt the familiar pull in his lower belly, his balls retracting, ready to release all they contained. Waiting for her signal, he felt her nails dig into his back, her strong lean thighs gripping his upper arms as she raised her ass off the bed to meet his thrusts. As she cried her release, he allowed himself to do the same, filling her with his hot seed.

Willa trailed kisses down his face as he freed her legs, letting them slide down his body to wrap around his waist. He settled between her thighs, his big forearms resting on either side of her head.

"I love you, Scott," she said tenderly.

"Love you more, Willa." He kissed her nose, pulling her to his side. "Get some sleep, baby. It's gonna be a long forty-eight hours." She was asleep before he could finish his sentence. He grinned but then realized if he were a gentleman, he would get up to wipe her clean, so she wouldn't wake up on a wet sheet. He tried to stand, but she held him to her.

"I'm just trying to clean you up, baby. I don't want you to wake up on a messy sheet." He could almost feel himself blush in the darkness. He'd never been so considerate of any woman.

"Don't you dare," she snarled, hugging him closer. "I love the feeling of you inside me, our passion dripping from me. I want to wake up remembering this." He could feel himself harden again and cursed his brainless dick.

"See," she grinned against his chest, "he agrees." Skull laughed as she trailed kisses down his chest. He knew where she was headed, and this time, he was going to make sure he got what he wanted as well. Lifting her easily, spinning her inconsequential weight, he spread her legs so his skilled tongue could have his dessert while she licked his lollipop.

"Fuck yes," he moaned against her swollen lips. His thick, heavy tongue flicked inside her sweetness. Letting his tongue circle her nub, he lapped up their passion and then dove in, tugging on her clit.

"Oh wow, you're really, wow, really good at this..." He felt her bucking against his face and knew his sweet Willa wouldn't last long, but then again, neither would he. That was his last coherent thought before his world exploded inside the pretty mouth of Willa Ross; her sweet lips magically took him to a place he'd never been, blissful, satisfied, unequivocal happiness.

Ten minutes later, he convinced her they both needed to rinse off and then crawled into the cool crisp sheets once again, both out before their heads hit the pillow.

CHAPTER THIRTY-TWO

"What do you mean he wasn't in the cage?" Craig's face scrunched in a fierce scowl, his anger filling his body from toes to fingers.

"I mean he wasn't there," said Edgars. "We checked the entire island. The cage was empty, and no one was on the island. Not your sister or the big fuck we threw overboard."

Matteo shifted nervously from one foot to the other. He knew when they found the island empty that they should have just cut their losses and run. If Kevin was alive and free, along with the sister and her big bodyguard, they were all in deep shit. It wouldn't be long before the authorities came after them, closely followed by the military. He would lose everything. His retirement, his benefits, and most-assuredly his freedom.

"They didn't walk off that island," said Craig. "How the fuck did they get away?"

"No idea, boss," said Matteo. "I think we need to..."

"What?" yelled Craig. "You think we need to what? You're so fucking smart; what is it you think we need to do? You had one job. Keep my brother on that island until I was ready for him to die. Now, he's out there somewhere, maybe dead, maybe alive. But if I were a betting man, I'd bet somehow my sister and that overgrown gnome made their way to the island."

"How did they get off?" asked Edgars.

"That's a great question," sneered Craig. Taking out his phone, he quickly dialed a number and waited. "Hey, Briggs! How's it hangin', brother?"

"Craig Ross, nice to hear from you," said the man stiffly.

"Listen, Briggs, I need a favor."

"Of course, you do," said the other man.

"My younger brother is missing; we've been looking for him for weeks. Intel said he might be in this area, and I was wondering if you or one of your stellar Coast Guardsman picked anyone up meeting his description?"

"Why would we *pick* someone up? I mean, why would the Coast Guard be your first call on this, Craig?" he asked suspiciously.

"You weren't my first call," lied Craig. "I just thought since it's Florida, and he doesn't swim well, maybe you guys got called out or something." The line was deathly quiet for a full thirty seconds, and Craig started to sweat, feeling the earth being pulled from beneath him.

"Nope, no rescues involving anyone named Ross in the last three weeks."

"Right, of course," said Craig with disbelief. "Thanks anyway." He hung up and realized the fatal error he'd made. He should have killed his sister and the hippy when he had the chance.

CHAPTER THIRTY-THREE

Dawn was breaking on the horizon; Skull was driving, Willa sound asleep in the back when his phone rang. Looking down, he smiled, knowing it was the call he suspected would come in.

"Briggs, what's up, brother?"

"Dickhead called just like you said," he chuckled. "Said his brother was missing and wasn't a good swimmer, worried he might have been in trouble, and we rescued him. Told him we hadn't rescued anyone named Ross in at least three weeks."

"Perfect," smirked Skull. "That will send him running back to Virginia, which is exactly what we want. I owe you one, Briggs."

"You owe me nothing, brother," he said confidently. "In case you forgot, you saved my fucking ugly ass on that little excursion near Haiti. My wife and daughters thank you."

"Happy I was there, Briggs. Come and see us in Virginia when you can."

"Will do, brother, will do." Ending the call, he thrummed his fingers against the steering wheel, deep in thought.

"You pegged him," smiled Blade. "You said he would reach out to the Guard if he thought you or Kevin were rescued."

"I know that he's the kind of man who attempts to make friends, or at least freinemies, with anyone he comes into touch with."

"Frienemies?"

"Yea, you know, enemies who act like friends or friends who sometimes act like enemies, frienemies." Blade nodded his head, chuckling. "We're only about four hours from the compound. I doubt Craig would fly but give Ghost a heads up."

Blade nodded, sending a long text to the team. If Skull was right, Craig would head toward Virginia and try to track down his sister and brother, which would lead him directly to the Steel Patriots compound and their family. Receiving an affirmative from Ghost, Blade turned to see the concern etched on Skull's features.

"He won't get to her, brother; you know we won't let that happen."

"I know, believe me, I know, but if what Ghost said is right about the ROL, we may have another issue on our hands as well. We have no idea how many women and children are in that compound and how many want to be there. I don't want to turn on the news and see another situation with burning buildings and dead kids, not on our watch anyway."

"You know that Ghost would never allow that," said Blade. "I'm sure he's working with Ivan right now on gathering intel on their compound. Combine that with whatever strange shit Ace is probably doing, and we'll know all there is to know about them."

Skull nodded once again, his gaze briefly drifting to the rear-view mirror, glancing at the sleeping face of Willa.

"If I lose her, I won't recover, Blade," he whispered. Blade gave a sharp jerk of his head and gripped his friend's shoulder.

"You. Will. Not. Lose her," he said between clenched teeth. "You have my word on that." He spotted a tear rolling down the cheek of his big friend and nearly lost his own check on his emotions. Their connection and love undeniable. Skull was right. If something happened to Willa, he would be inconsolable. Blade would not allow that to happen. He knew what that felt like. He knew the indelible mark that left on your soul, the wound that never, ever healed.

"I'm trying to figure out the connection of Craig to the ROL. I mean, why would he hook up with a bunch of polygamists? It just doesn't make sense. I'm sure they're paying him a fair price for the women and the weapons, but as sick as the world is, he could make more money elsewhere."

"I agree," said Blade. "It doesn't make sense. What's his pull to the ROL?"

"A woman?" questioned Skull.

"Maybe, but again, what about a man?" Skull chuckled, then tilted his head questioningly.

"I think that's the wrong brother, but stranger things have occurred. We still don't know how he got Kevin involved in the first place. I mean, if Adam is right, he was forcing Kevin to be a part of his plans or somehow tricking him into helping him."

"Yea, well, only Kevin is going to be able to help us with that issue."

"I'm hungry," came the small voice from the backseat.

"Christ, woman! Is that all you do? Eat?" smiled Blade.

"Nope," she said, leaning over the seat to kiss Skull's cheek, "just ask my very happy boyfriend." His face flamed red, and Blade laughed so hard he thought he might crack a rib. No woman had ever been able to make Skull blush, and this tiny little thing seemed to make a regular habit of it.

"Now, are you going to feed me before I get hangry?"

"I damn sure don't want to see you hangry, baby," said Skull. "There are a few places at the next exit. We'll stop for a little while and sit and eat. I'm tired of fast food." A few minutes later, they were pulling into the parking lot of a large breakfast chain.

Finding a booth by the window, they ordered their food and waited.

"You know," said Willa, "I was thinking about the watches you guys wear with the GPS tracking on them."

"Yea?" asked Skull.

"Yea, I mean, I understand the GPS software and the tracking that's being used, but I was thinking I might be able to write a program that would allow your tech guy, Ace is it?" Blade and Skull nodded. "Ace to not only track you guys, but anyone who was nearby that had tracking on their phones or GPS systems, and that data would be entered in the system as well."

"Wait, I don't understand. Why you would do that?" said Blade.

"Well, let's say he tracked you guys in a crowded marketplace in Istanbul," said Willa. Blade and Skull straightened. They were certain that Willa didn't know how close to the truth her story was, but it still made them nervous. "Let's just say that you disappeared. He has your last known location at the marketplace. Somehow your GPS is turned off or broken. I think, with the right software, Ace would be able to find those who were in the same vicinity and perhaps track and follow them to determine your last location or maybe what happened to you. Basically, I can make your signal attach to another and follow it."

"A software program could do that?" said Skull.

"Definitely," she smiled. "That and so much more! I could probably improve on the GPS system he's using now, even mirroring the terrain to his computer. Again, if you disappeared, he might be able to see mountains or villages nearby. Or let's say the island we were on. He would have been able to ping against Craig or the other two men's phones and trace them."

"Trace them? Is that legal?" asked Blade.

"I don't know the answer to that," laughed Willa, "you're the geniuses in that department. But I'd sure be willing to develop it if Ghost gave his approval, and Ace was okay with it."

"Ace? Why would you want his approval?"

"Tech geeks are super protective of the things they develop. There's a lot of piracy in our industry. I'm guessing that Ace has developed everything you guys are using from the ground up. I would never want him to feel like I'm infringing on his territory."

"That's pretty considerate of you, Willa," said Skull. "I think once you get to know Ace, you'll discover he really doesn't have an ego. He's willing to share his technology with just about anyone as long as it's for good."

"Awesome! I'll speak to Ghost and Ace when we get settled." Skull nodded his head, a grin sliding across his face. Willa was planning long-term to work with the team at the compound and, hopefully, with him.

"So, Willa, what will you do with your apartment when you get back?" asked Blade. Skull nearly spit his water across the table, giving his friend the evil eye.

"Oh, well, I need to get it cleaned out, I suppose. There's really nothing I can save. To be honest," she said, glancing sideways at Skull, "I don't want to go back there." Skull exhaled the breath he'd been holding.

"Then don't," he said, turning to stare at her. "Don't go back. You have a place with us... with me. We can stay at the cottage or..."

"Yes!" she said, practically leaping into his lap. "Yes, I'll stay with you at the cottage or in your room in the barn or in a tent. Yes, I'll stay with you, Scott, anywhere you are." He chuckled at her enthusiasm, kissing her soundly in front of the entire restaurant and his best friend.

"You done eating yet?" Blade asked the woman.

"No, but I can wrap up the rest of the sandwich and the cookies and take them to go." The two men could only laugh, watching her wrap the last scraps of food in a napkin. Leaving enough cash for the bill and a generous tip, they loaded up and headed north once again.

Almost exactly four hours later, they pulled into the Steel Patriots compound, tired, road-weary, and hungry again. George threw together a quick meal as they all gathered in the restaurant.

"Where's my brother?" asked Willa. "I need to see him."

"No need to worry," said the faint voice behind her. Turning, she saw a tall, handsome, sandy-haired man with his arms wrapped around her brother's waist. "I'm right here, sis, safe and sound."

CHAPTER THIRTY-FOUR

"Are you sure you're feeling well enough to be out of bed?" she asked again, brushing the black hair from his eyes. Kevin rolled his eyes, Adam chuckled by his side.

"Wil, seriously, you're driving me crazy," he laughed. "I'm fine. I need to eat. I need to drink lots of water, but I'm going to be fine. Just ask that stunningly gorgeous doctor with the eyes that would turn even my head, taking care of me."

"You better be glad you bat for the other team, little man," said the booming bass voice from behind him. Willa, Adam, and Kevin all jumped slightly. "That stunningly gorgeous doctor is my wife. But I agree with you. She's damn fine." Zulu winked at the threesome and smiled.

"Shit, he's scary," said Adam, watching the big man move toward Gabi. He pulled his wife in for a big hug and kiss, rubbing the top of one of the twins' heads.

"He's a sweetheart," said Willa. "They all are. They've bent over backwards for me, done so much, I don't think I can ever repay any of them. I'm happy here, Kevin."

"No!" he feigned disbelief. "You're happy being catered to and guarded by a big, gorgeous, handsome man? I mean, seriously, Willa, who would be happy with that?" He smiled at his sister. Adam nudged him gently.

"You're such a jerk, you know. I don't know how you put up with him, Adam," she said with tears in her eyes. "I missed you. I was so worried about you. Scott, he just kept assuring me that we would find you."

"He seems like a good man, sis."

"He is, Kevin. He's the best. I fell in love with him almost immediately. I don't understand how. I mean, I just walked into the garage wanting to see the bike, and there he was, this larger-than-life character. He was so handsome and strong. It's scary and overwhelming and…"

"Wonderful?" said Adam, smiling at her.

"Yes, wonderful." Willa grinned at her brother and his partner. "I'm happy for you two also, you know. I hate that you didn't feel comfortable enough to tell me sooner, Kevin. I would have loved to have been a part of your life with Adam."

"You will be. From now on, no more secrets." He smiled at Adam and then gave a gentle hug to his sister.

"Agreed, although we seem to have one big secret that no one can figure out," said Willa, watching as Skull, Ghost, Ace, Blade, and Whiskey came toward them. "I'm guessing you want to talk about our brother."

"I'm afraid we have to, Willa," said Ghost. "Are you feeling up to it, Kevin?"

"I'm good, really. Thanks to the beautiful, uh, the big man's gorgeous wife," he grinned. "Thanks to Gabi, I'm really okay. And if I keep eating all that food George is making, I'll be overweight at my next physical. Although it looks as though I may be up for court-martial."

"We'll make sure that doesn't happen, brother," said Whiskey. Kevin nodded, emotions making their way to the surface as Adam gripped his hand beneath the table. Whiskey watched the interaction, something inside him slightly pissed that they felt the need to hide their affection for one another. He knew the criticism they must have faced in the Army, but he decided to speak up.

"You don't have to hide from us. We know you're a couple, and none of us give a shit, brother. You're both one of us. You've served honorably, and that's all we care about. Love doesn't care who you are or what sex you are. Don't hide your love from us; we're family, and family doesn't keep secrets."

"You have no idea what that means to us," said Adam. Whiskey simply nodded as the others gave a nod in their direction as well.

"First," said Ace, taking a seat near Willa and Kevin, "I need you to tell us what these photographs are. They make no sense at all."

"I have no clue," said Willa, looking at her brother.

"They're pictures of my home," said Kevin. "Mine and Adam's. Each one of those locations has something hidden in it from the shipments my brother stole. Firing pins, codes for the launchers, blasting caps, anything I could remove quickly and easily to ensure that they weren't going to function, I did."

"Fucking genius," laughed Skull. "That's awesome, brother, but weren't you worried that if he hacked into that file, he would know what that was?"

"Nope," said Kevin, shaking his head. "My brother hasn't visited our home, ever. Adam and I moved in together almost two years ago. Craig never came to my home. He may have known where I was living, but he didn't set foot in the house, so he wouldn't know what any of this was. I knew what I was doing, and I hoped that Wil would figure it out before he got to it. Adam had no clue; the less he knew, the better."

"Why didn't you report this?" asked Ghost.

"Donan thinks Craig walks on water. Willa can tell you that Craig is a master manipulator. He did it when our parents were alive as well, always coming out the other end of any situation looking like the doting, protective brother. He was careful with Willa because of her age and size that he didn't do anything completely awful, but spying on her was enough to make me nervous. My brother was able to convince Donan that I was nothing but a fucking screwup. When he found a way to get me transferred to Bragg, I knew I was in deep shit. It started with him threatening Adam, and then it was Willa. When I refused to buy into all of that, he made sure my career was jeopardized. The last shipment that came in, I refused to help him, so he drugged me and took everything. It made me look as though I were asleep on duty. If I went to get a drug screen, it would look as though I was using drugs. Lose-lose for me."

"What about the fight in the bar, the last one?" asked Skull.

"Yea, I was trying to get him to see how much danger he was putting Willa in. I found the e-mails between him and the elders at the ROL. He thought he was so smart, but I hacked into his e-mail account and found the communications. Craig was thinking about selling Willa to them."

"Oh my God," she said, holding her stomach. "He was going to sell me. My own brother?"

"I'm sorry, Wil. He said the elders were willing to pay big money for you. I wasn't going to let him take you. I was hoping to make him lash out at me at the bar. Unfortunately, he knows my Achilles."

"Adam," said Blade.

"Yea. He said he'd make his life a living hell, make sure I was dishonorably discharged, effectively ruining his reputation as well."

"It won't happen, brother," said Ghost. "I've already sent documentation to General Donan and asked him to do nothing right now with Craig. If he contacts him, I've told him that he should notify us and Ivan Pechkin. I also told him if he doesn't, he will be in collusion with your brother and effectively brought up on charges of interference with a federal investigation."

"You said all those big words by yourself?" laughed Blade.

"Fuck you, asshole. I got some help from Kat." The table let out a loud chuckle, and Ghost shook his head.

"So now what do we do?" asked Willa.

"*We* do nothing," said Skull. "You will stay here with your brother and be safe. We will find out what's happening at the ROL and decide what our next move will be." Whiskey disconnected the call he was on and spoke to the group.

"Ivan has three men going down to Kevin and Adam's house to retrieve the evidence. Once we have that, Craig won't be able to hide any longer. My guess is he can't get his money from the ROL unless he can produce what you all took from him."

"He'll be angry," said Kevin. "He was already angry when he was torturing me."

"Yea, but you beat him," said Skull, gripping the man's shoulder. "You faced the fucking devil. You were tortured, and you beat him." Kevin nodded, emotion welling within him.

A gut-wrenching scream could be heard from behind the table, and every man stood, effectively forming a barrier around Willa and her brother, Adam joining in with the team. But it wasn't Craig or some other nefarious demon. It was the bulging Tinley.

"Oh shit!" yelled Eagle. "Someone find Gabi and Doc!"

"Uhhhhh!" yelled Tinley.

"Come on, baby. Let's get you upstairs to the treatment room," said Eagle sweetly, gripping the elbow of his screaming wife.

"No, nope, not happening. They're coming now!" she yelled. The men all stood stone-still, and Willa looked at them exasperated.

"Oh, for goodness' sake! Scott, Scott?! Go get Gabi and Doc. Blade? Go get the other wives. Ghost? I need blankets and tablecloths. Now!" she yelled. Kneeling beside the trembling Tinley, she held a gentle hand behind her head and one on her stomach.

"Hi, Tinley," she smiled, "nice to see you again. Okay, sweetie, you're going to be okay. I've taken a bunch of first-aid classes, which doesn't mean a lot, but I'll be here to help when the doc arrives."

"O-okay," she said, gasping for air. "Ty, Ty, I love you."

"I love you too, baby. I'm so proud of you. I'm right here," he said through tears. Seconds later, Gabi knelt at her feet, pushing up her skirt to check her cervix. Eagle rushed to be near his brother, Keegan seated close to her mother's head.

"Alright then, Tinley, it seems these three want to arrive now," said Gabi. "Let's go, Daddy, like we practiced. Help her breathe. George? I need hot water and clean towels. Doc? You got the kit?"

"Right here," he said, kneeling next to Gabi.

"Oooooo! Now! I need to push now!" yelled Tinley.

"Okay, now it is," said Gabi. "Push, honey, I see a full head of hair. Push!" Tinley bore down against the pain, the first little head, then the shoulders, and finally, their first child—a boy.

"It's a boy, Mama and Daddy," said Doc, grinning at his teammate. The next two came like they were shot from a cannon. All three babies were a little over five pounds, all perfectly healthy, thirty fingers, thirty toes, six eyes, three noses, three perfect little mouths, and one exhausted mama.

An hour later, they were safely in the treatment room upstairs. The three babies were checked and re-checked. Mama was resting comfortably. Eagle couldn't believe it, three boys. He had three sons. Somewhere in the back of his mind, he prayed that when his brother had children, it would be all girls. Hawk deserved that after his trail of broken hearts within the female population, prior to Keegan, of course.

"Have you thought of names?" asked Darby.

"We have," said Tinley, smiling sweetly at the room full of people. "The first born will be named after his daddy, Tyran Eagle O'Neal." The room smiled, watching the emotions cross Eagle's face.

"Baby number two," said Eagle, grinning, "will be Hawk Gunner O'Neal."

"Oh shit," said Gunner with an open mouth. "You named him after me?"

"I'm first," smiled Hawk through tears for his brother. "Thank you, Tinley, brother."

"Baby number three," said Tinley, "is Benjamin Scott O'Neal. Ty, Hawk, and Ben. Three strong names for three strong boys." Skull and Blade both raised their heads, complete shock filling their faces.

"I don't understand," whispered Blade.

"It's pretty simple," smiled Tinley. "You two have watched over me like mother hens. When I was in the garage, you made sure I was taken care of, fed, relaxed. Anything I needed, you were there. I cannot think of better godparents than the two of you for Ben." They both could only smile as Eagle handed Ben to Blade first. He held the tiny bundle for just a moment, and then quickly handed him off to Scott, who cradled the nearly weightless infant protectively in his big hands.

"Hi there," he said, looking down at the face of the helpless child, "I'm your Uncle Skull, and I'm gonna build you the coolest bike when you're old enough." The entire room chuckled at that as the children were passed around to their namesakes and then finally nestled back in their beds.

"Okay, everyone," said Gabi, "Mama needs her rest, and the babies need sleep. Out you go. Eagle? Don't leave her side. She'll need help getting up to use the bathroom. If she's hungry, let her eat what she wants right now. I'll be around. Just call me or Doc if you need anything at all." As they

filtered out of the room, Willa leaned into Skull.

"You're gonna make a great daddy one day, Scott."

Smiling down at her, he thought to himself, damn straight I am, just like my Pops.

CHAPTER THIRTY-FIVE

"Did you find the building manager?" asked Craig.

"No, he lives off-site. The apartment is still the same as it was when we left it. Nothing's been removed or taken. If your brother left something there, it was small," said Edgars.

"Listen, boss," said Matteo, "I'm all for getting paid and shit, but we've hit a dead-end here. Your sister is either dead or in the wind with her bodyguard; your brother obviously escaped and is out there and can pin us to everything. Don't you think it would be wise to head south now?"

Craig stared at the shattered room. Turning slowly, he faced the other two men, a sneer crossing his lips.

"You want to leave two million on the table?" he asked the men. "You want to just walk away from the final payout before we need to leave this shithole? Well, I don't! I want my money, and the only way I'm going to get it is to find the shit my brother took from me. I just know Willa is the key to all this. We find her, we find my brother and the answers to where everything went."

"What about the ROL? They're losing patience with us. Elder John contacted me this morning, and he wasn't happy," said Matteo. "He said if we didn't produce the stuff, they weren't going to pay for any of it. Said he could find a better source for women and everything else they need."

Feeling the rage build within him, Craig slammed a fist into Matteo's face. The other man stumbled backward, grabbing his jaw. He was surprised he didn't fall, shocked really. Matteo stood straight, staring Craig down.

"Hit me again," he growled, "and you'll see why I was the top marksman in my unit."

"Fuck you," said Craig. "I don't need either one of you." Edgars looked at Matteo, his eyebrows slowly riding up his forehead. Shrugging, he turned toward the door.

"Where the hell are you going?"

"You don't need us, remember?" said Edgars. "You've lost it, Craig. I don't know what's really going on here, but you've got a hard-on for this last payout and doing as much harm to your brother and sister as you possibly can. I don't need any of it. I have enough money for my little place in the sun. You're a fucking psycho, and I've had enough."

"Me too," said Matteo. "I'm done. Time to see mi familia. Let's go."

"Fucking cowards!" yelled Craig as they walked out the door. "You're both fucking cowards! I don't need either one of you!" Kicking the tattered footstool across the room, he shoved shattered photographs off the sofa and plopped down.

He knew it was here. Something in this apartment would tell him where Kevin and Willa were hiding. Looking around the space, he smiled. At least Edgars and Matteo did something right. They really trashed this place good.

Slowly picking his way through the garbage, he made his way toward the bedroom she used as an office. He remembered setting up the desk for her, those precious computers the only thing she really cared about. Files were scattered everywhere, information on the sale of her software, all the zeros making his head spin. He wanted that money; he deserved that money.

Kicking the piles of folders in frustration, he started to head for the door when one stood out. It was a simple manila folder with a name on it. His name.

"What the hell is this?" he asked, picking it up.

Inside were photos of a motorcycle, rudimentary sketches of various designs, and copies of e-mails sent back and forth to a motorcycle shop.

"Steel Garage," he murmured, looking at the name. Opening his phone, he searched the name, and there it was. Plain as the nose on his face.

"Well, well, well, baby sister was going to give me a gift. Well, fuck your motorcycle, sis, but I will take the address of the bike shop. I'm coming for you."

CHAPTER THIRTY-SIX

"Why are we staying in the barn and not the cottage?" asked Willa. "I mean, it doesn't really matter to me. I just love our little cottage. I have good memories there." She gave him a wink, and he laughed, hugging her close.

"Just to be safe, baby," said Skull, kissing her temple. "Until Craig is found, we want both you and Kevin inside. You can go down to the restaurant, but no further. If he tries to contact you…"

"I know, I know, don't answer it," she grinned. Skull nodded but pulled her toward him onto his lap.

"Listen, Willa, I know this is a lot to ask of both of you, but our primary concern right now is for your safety and Kevin's. We have the evidence that was in his and Adam's home. That alone is enough to put Craig in prison for life. If he's panicked, and I think he will be, he'll find you and find a way to come here. I won't let him touch you, baby, ever, but I need you to do your part in this as well and follow our rules."

"I love you, Scott," she whispered into his neck. "I love you so much it hurts. I just want all of this to be over with and for us to live our life. A life here with your friends and teammates. I've come to think of these people as family, and I'm hoping they'll learn to think of me as the same."

"They already do, baby girl," he said, kissing her. "Love you too, Willa. I never thought I'd have my chance at a happily ever after. Then you walked into that garage, and my heart nearly shattered with joy. When all this is done, I want to invite my folks down here to meet you."

"I'd love that," she said with tears in her eyes. Kissing her once again, he stood with her in his arms, earning him a squeal of delight from her sweet lips.

"Gotta go make magic bikes, baby. Don't leave the building. I'll come back up here for lunch." She nodded, kissing him once more and then following him downstairs to the hustle and bustle of the kitchen. Blade was already grabbing a breakfast sandwich, his coffee mug steaming as he walked past them.

"Morning, Tinkerbell," he grinned.

"Morning, Master Chief," she giggled.

"Master Chief?" came the echo from the room.

"Inside joke," said Blade. "Tink over there knows a game developer. When I said she looked like Tinkerbell, she joked that I wouldn't want to be called Master Chief or Aquaman. Told her she was mistaken. Both are compliments to me."

"Sweet!" said Hawk. "You know a game developer? That's pretty cool, Willa."

"He's a college friend. Lives in Silicon Valley and works for a major game developer. I don't understand half the stuff he does, but apparently, it's wildly popular." Ace walked in carrying one of his many laptops, Charlie with an arm around his waist. Kissing his cheek, she moved to sit with the other women.

"Okay, everyone," said Ace, turning the laptop to the room. "For those of you who don't know, this is Craig Ross. I've just sent his photograph to everyone on their phones. If you see him, do not engage. Send a message through our regular channels to Ghost, Whiskey, or Skull. Skull? You need to stay inside the garage today. He knows your face and Blade's. Make sure you're out of sight."

"Got it," he smiled. Ace's transformation still made them pause. Charlie was grinning in his direction with the admiration of a woman madly in love. It's what gave Skull the courage to pursue Willa, and he was damn sure going to let Ace know that.

"Is that a bad man?" asked Calla.

"He is, honey," said Gunner. "If you see him, don't say anything. Just tell one of us, okay?"

"Okay, Daddy," she said, leaping into his arms, kissing his face.

"Okay, people, we have a business to run. Let's go," said Ghost.

CHAPTER THIRTY-SEVEN

Craig followed the winding mountain road toward the Steel Garage. The trees were in full bloom, the summer sun filtering light across the roadway with a kaleidoscope of color. Some other time, he might actually stop and enjoy the spectacular views of the mountains and the valley below. It was certainly a picturesque little place.

He saw the sign for Steel Garage ahead and pulled through the big chain-link fence and gate, open for all patrons today. Noticing the big red barn, he stared upward to see the sign Club Steel. Whoever these guys were, they owned a shit ton of property and were definitely making the best of it.

Pulling his car to a stop, he stepped from the vehicle to see a little girl of about six running around, skipping rope as she did. Perfect.

"Hi there," he said, smiling his best 'I'm friendly' smile. The little girl turned, stopping her rope as she did. She stared at him for a moment but said nothing. "I'm sorry if I scared you. I just wondered if you could tell me if there's a girl here named Willa."

"I'm not 'posed to talk to strangers," she said.

"Okay, that's smart," he grinned, fighting back his anger. "Is there another adult here who might help me?"

"My daddy," she said, smiling. "He works at the gym."

"That's awesome. Can you get your daddy for me?" he asked. Her head bobbed an affirmative, the long brown curls bouncing down her back. Her little legs took off running toward the garage, and Craig looked around the property. A few minutes later, several patrons began coming out of the barn, and he scanned each face, looking for Willa or Kevin. He saw two men laughing as they walked around the property and thought it was curious, but nothing seemed out of the ordinary. Then he heard the little girl come from behind him.

"Hey, mister," she cried out.

"Hey, pretty girl," said the spider to the fly. "Is your daddy coming?"

"Yep, he said you should wait in the res'rant. His hands are dirty, so he's washing them, and then he'll be in there. The ice cream sundae is my favorite if you're hungry." Craig couldn't help but chuckle at her childlike enthusiasm.

"I just might order that," he said. "Thanks for your help."

Now, it was time to find his bitch of a sister and that little queen, his brother. Opening the trunk, he tucked the pistol into his waist at his back. Never hurts to be careful. He was going to get what he came for and then make his way to West Virginia and get his money.

Years of his life were wasted on the two of them. He was done worrying about others instead of himself. Done. When this was over, he would be sitting on the beach somewhere sipping Pina Coladas with pretty senorita's waiting on him hand and foot.

Yes, indeed, he deserved this.

Opening the big double doors, he stepped inside the brightly lit room. A young woman was behind the bar and looked up, smiling at him.

"Hi there," she grinned. "I'm Amanda. Sit wherever you like, and someone will be there soon to take your order." He nodded, taking note of the nice tits on the girl. She might be his next gift to the ROL.

Taking a seat at a small table with his back to the wall where he could see the big double doors at the front and the big steel door along the back wall, he waited patiently for a waiter, or if he were lucky enough, to see Kevin or Willa. Instead, he nearly shit his pants when the big bodyguard walked in, followed by three more men all about the same size.

"Hello, Craig," said Skull. "Long time no see, buddy. Did you miss me?"

"How the fuck…"

"How the fuck indeed," grinned Skull. If you thought Skull looked scary with a passive face, grinning, he looked deranged and damned near untouchable. "You tried to hurt Kevin and Willa. My Willa."

"Y-your Willa?" he stammered. "She doesn't have a boyfriend. I would know. Besides, I'm her brother. There's an explanation for all of this. Kevin took–"

"-your firing pins, and codes, and anything else I could to stop you," said Kevin, walking toward them. He was dressed in blue jeans and a sweatshirt, looking thin but very much alive.

"You're alive," whispered Craig.

"Yea, asshole. I'm alive. You tried to kill me and Willa. You're going down, Craig, in a flying fuck of flames. The information I had has been recovered and sent to the FBI, Army CIC, and General Donan. His golden boy is seriously tarnished."

"You bastard!" he growled.

"Uh, pot meet kettle," said Skull, grinning. He took a step forward, his big body casting a shadow over Craig's smaller frame. "You're lucky I don't kill you right here. Try to fucking hurt my woman again, and you'll die a seriously painful death." Craig eyed the big man up and down, glancing around him to see the other them.

"You're not just some hippy, are you?" he asked. Skull grinned. "Who are you? I deserve to know that." Ghost stepped forward.

"Eric 'Ghost' Stanton, U.S. Navy SEAL, retired. This is my team of SEALs, MARSOC, Rangers, Green Berets, Delta, and," he said, grinning at Skull, "Coast Guard."

"Shit," murmured Craig.

"CIC is on their way, but before they get here, you're going to tell us why and how you're connected with the ROL," said Ghost. He looked at the room of men, stopping at the face of his brother. It was disgusting how Adam stood protectively over him. It made his stomach roll.

"Money. It was all about money and pussy," he grinned. The force at which Skull's fist connected to his nose sent him flying backwards against the wall, his body slumping to the floor. It took him a minute to regain his sense of direction and balance, but he stood, wiping the blood from his face.

"Fine, fine, you want the story. Here it is. The elders approached me about luring women to the complex. I basically gave the women a little something to come with me compliantly, and then I spent a few days alone with them training them, the hard way."

"You're not a man," said Kevin.

"Neither are you," he sneered. Skull started toward him again, but it was Adam that stepped forward, slamming his fist into his face. The blood gushed forward as he cussed, gripping his face.

"Fuck! Okay! It was easy. Women would go anywhere with a man in uniform. They were all lost, no families, just looking for something. A little coaxing from me, and they were easy prey. Pop out a few babies, and..."

"And what?" asked Ghost.

"Look, when they were done with the women, they either killed them or sold them off. The elders want to make sure they're armed if the feds decide to get to them. Me? I don't really give a shit either way, but they're pretty determined to have the weapons. Problem is brother dear fucked me over, and I need to get what they paid for." All the men started toward him, but Craig took the moment

to pull the pistol from his waistband, pointing it directly at Kevin. "I'm not going with CIC."

"You're right. You're not," said Blade, pointing to the upper balcony window. The long rifle of

Hawk was pointed directly at Craig, the bright dot on his chest. He gave a wink and a wave, grinning at

the man. Apparently, Craig was long on stupidity and short on common sense as he started to pull the

trigger. Hawk was quicker. The echoing of the big rifle in the restaurant ringing in their ears.

Craig dropped the gun, his arm now dripping in blood from the bullet wound, the pain forcing

him to his knees as Skull kicked the gun out of his reach.

"Why are you all doing this?" he grimaced.

"Easy," said the small voice behind the crowd. Willa walked toward them, lightly gripping her

brother's arm as she passed him and Adam, then stopping next to Skull, wrapping an arm around his

waist. "For love, something you will never understand." Skull grinned, turning to walk away from the

mess. Ghost looked around the group of men and started delivering orders.

"Doc? Wrap him up. We need him alive for CIC. Whiskey? Call Ivan and let him know about

the ROL. If they need help with the kids, tell him to let us know. We'll get them somewhere safe."

Whiskey was already speaking to Ivan as he walked away.

Gunner and Tango secured him to the chair while Doc wrapped up the arm. Willa sat with

Adam, Kevin, and Skull, watching the flurry of activity happen.

Skull could almost read her thoughts. Despite his actions, he was still her brother and provided

for her growing up. She eyed him from across the room, staring hard.

"Honey, it's normal to feel bad for him," he said, rubbing her back.

"I don't feel bad for him, but I also don't believe him when he says it's all about the money. It's bullshit. I would have given him millions if he wanted it. This makes no sense at all." Willa stood and started to walk toward Craig. Skull wanted to reach out and pull her back but knew he was secured and unable to harm her. Kevin and Adam followed her.

"Why?" she asked. Craig let a grin slip, staring at her.

"Told you, little sis, money."

"I'm not your little sister. Why? You had more than enough money, and you knew I would give you whatever you wanted. Why?"

"Believe it or not, makes no difference to me," he said, looking away. Willa stared at him, glancing at his face; his eyes avoided her own as she ran possible scenarios through her head.

"It's the ROL. You were born into the ROL," she said. The entire room stopped what they were doing, Ghost and Skull staring open-mouthed at Willa.

"How... how did you know that?" said Craig, turning ashen.

"I'm the computer expert, remember? I've been trying to track down our biological parents for years. I couldn't find anything about Kevin and me, but you... you I could track back to the U.S. to a mother that took a plane to Bangkok, lived there for almost a year, and then disappeared." Craig tried to stand, tried to reach out to her.

"Shut up! Don't you talk about my mother!" He squirmed in his seat, trying to break free of the restraints.

"So, what happened? She got pregnant with you and changed her mind about the ROL? Did they find her?" Craig said nothing, but his silence only allowed Willa to finally put the pieces together.

"That's it, isn't it. Your mother got pregnant and changed her mind. Trying to escape the ROL, she went as far as she could, but my guess is they found her."

"Shut up!" he screamed again. His breathing was rapid, his face sweating now. "Yes! Yes, they found her and discovered a black baby, not one of their precious white babies like the elders. I have no clue if she was pregnant when she got there or got pregnant after, but they didn't want her or me. They dumped me in that orphanage and killed my mother."

"But why are you doing this? Why are you helping them? The weapons." Craig grinned at his naïve sister, knowing that she would never understand his motives.

"Fuck me," whispered Eagle, "you wanted this to turn into another national media circus. You wanted them to burn to the ground."

"Bingo," smiled Craig. "I was going to give them what they wanted and then anonymously let the feds know. Those crazy elders would never allow the women and kids to be taken. They'd rather kill them all. Fucking crazy old men."

"Those are innocent women and children," gasped Willa.

"They're not innocent. Those whores all approached me at bars. Some took a little coaxing, but they were more than willing to spread their legs. They weren't innocent. No one is," said Craig cynically.

"Warn Ivan and the fed team. They're going to need to move in with caution," said Ghost. Craig shook his head, grinning at them.

"It won't matter. They'll all die today. My promise to my mother fulfilled."

CHAPTER THIRTY-EIGHT

CIC arrived two hours later, Craig all tied up in a nice bow for them. They didn't have to do anything except cart him off with the bucket load of evidence gathered by the Steel Patriots. Following them into the barn was General Donan. Adam and Kevin watched him speaking with Ghost and Skull, his face flushing a bright red as he spoke. Turning, he moved toward their table. Both men stood.

"General," said Kevin. "You'll have to forgive me, but I'm not feeling well." Kevin tried to exit the room, but the general gripped his upper arm, holding him in place.

"Hear me out, Ross. Please." Kevin nodded, taking his seat once again. "I'm sorry for believing your brother and not you or Lt. Schumer. It's prompted me to make a career decision. I'll be retiring, effective immediately. You and Lt. Schumer will have no actions brought against you at all. Your record will be expunged of any activities your brother had a hand in. You will receive your appropriate rank and back pay."

"That's quite an admission by the Army," said Kevin sarcastically.

"It was quite an error," grinned Donan. "You two will also be allowed your choice of duty stations... together."

"I want to go back to Andrews," said Kevin. "I need to be close to my sister."

"I'd like to be transferred there as well," said Adam.

"Done," he said, reaching out a big hand to the two men. "I really am sorry about this. Your brother had a lot of people fooled, but it was my mistake for not following through on the investigations."

"Thank you for saying that." He nodded, placing his hat back on his head, and turned to head out the door. Willa smiled at her brother and his partner, reaching for his hand and giving it a good squeeze.

"It's done," said Willa. "We can live the life we're supposed to now."

"I love you, Willa," said Kevin, "but it's going to be months of appearing in court for Craig, depositions, hearings, sentencing. It will be a long year."

"Yea, but we'll be together, all of us," she said, looking at Adam and Skull.

Blade watched the chaos around him. CIC carted Craig away, the general with his tail tucked between his legs followed. Adam and Kevin looked happy. Skull definitely looked happy, staring at the little Tinkerbell perched on his knee. They were all with who they should be. Happy and living the life intended for them.

He remembered a life like that. A life where he was supposed to live happily ever after. Young and home on leave, he finally sought out the girl that plagued his dreams. Dating since high school, Samantha Doiron was the stuff of wet dreams and posters for bedroom walls. Full hips, big round tits, doe eyes, and a mouth made for sin. Now that he was established in one place with an off-base apartment, he would finally ask her to marry him.

Except things are never quite what they seem. Samantha didn't answer her phone, so he went to her parents' home only to find her little sister, Susie. She didn't know where her sister was and asked him to stay, except he couldn't. He needed to find Sam. He did notice that something about little Susie was different than when he'd seen her three years ago. She was taller, prettier, more confident somehow.

He searched half the night for Samantha, finally entering one of the many backwoods bars littering the bayous he called home, and there she was. Seated at the bar, her tongue down the throat of Richie Blanchard, her skirt hiked up nearly to her hips, his hands feeling his way around her luscious curves. Calming his temper, he walked slowly toward the two when Samantha finally looked up.

"Bennie! What are you doing here?" she said, smiling and jumping off the stool into his arms as if nothing were wrong. He pushed her back.

"I told you I was coming home," he said. "Richie. Nice to see you."

"Nice to see you, Ben. Sorry about this. Thought Sam told you we were engaged."

"Engaged? No, she didn't tell me that." He turned his gaze to Samantha, waiting for an explanation.

"Don't know what you want from me, Bennie…"

"Don't call me that. My name is Ben, Benjamin, or Blade."

"Blade?" she scoffed. "Whatever. You ran off to play toy soldier, and I was alone. A girl has needs." Blade nodded at the couple, noticing the apologetic look on Richie's face.

"Well, then. Good luck." Turning on his heels, he went back into the parking lot, only to run smack into Susie Doiron. "You followin' me, Susie Q?"

"N-no… I just… are you okay?" she asked.

"Will be," he said, side-stepping her. "See ya later, Susie Q. Take care." He watched her in his rear-view mirror, the neon lights of the old bar at her back as she lifted a small hand to wave at him. It was the last time he'd been back home, except for the twenty-four hours to attend his mother's funeral.

Searching the happy faces of his teammates, he nodded, turning to head back to work. What else could he do?

CHAPTER THIRTY-NINE

Six months later...

"Craig was found guilty on all charges," said Kat, addressing the group at dinner. "He'll be court-martialed, sent to Leavenworth on two life sentences. He was charged with twenty-two counts of accessory to murder, given that his ultimate plan played out with the ROL. Eight women, ten children, and four men, all dead."

"I'm glad it's over," said Willa, snuggling into Scott's side. The snow was coming down heavily, and with only three days to Christmas, they were scrambling to make sure everything was ready for the children. Scott would be playing Santa Claus, and the others were making reindeer and sleigh tracks in the snow. Willa looked up to see Blade coming in the door. He stomped his feet, snow dropping off his big boots, as he wiped the flakes from his hair.

As he always did, he walked by the table and kissed the top of her head, and then nudged Skull in the arm.

"When are you gonna marry Tink?" asked Blade.

"Blade! That's not nice," said Willa. "We'll get married when we both feel it's the right time." The others all smiled in their direction as Skull stood, then kneeled in front of her.

"Willa?"

"Wh-what are you doing?" she whispered.

"If I have to explain it, I might already be in trouble." He chuckled and then reached into his pocket, pulling out the biggest diamond she'd ever seen. "Willa Ross, I love you more than anything or anyone in my life. I don't deserve you, but I will damn sure do everything in my power to make you happy. Will you please, please, consent to becoming my wife?" Willa could no longer hold back the tears, nodding profusely.

"Yes, yes!" she cried as he placed the ring on her tiny finger. "I love you so much, Scott. You're my everything, everything! Well, you and one other man."

"Kevin?" he grinned. She shook her head. "What the fuck, Willa! Who..." She grinned as she rubbed her belly.

"A baby boy, Daddy. Due in June. I was going to make it your Christmas present, but you need to know you're marrying two people here," she grinned. "Are you happy?" Skull said nothing for several seconds, then did what no one had ever seen him do. He cried like a baby.

"So fucking happy," he said into her neck, picking her up to gently hug her. George brought out the food for a pre-Christmas celebration, and the conversation was loud, as always. Just as they were about to lock the doors for the holidays, the wind blew in, snow following the bundled individual.

"Hi there," called Amanda, "we were just about to close up. Can I help you?"

"I'm looking for Benjamin LeBlanc?" said the sweet, southern voice. Blade lifted his head in recognition. What the fuck?

"Susie Doiron. What the fucking hell are you doing here?"

"Nice to see you too, Ben."

EXCERPT from BLADE

"I promise I'll be back soon, Sam," he said, zipping up his jeans. "I have basic, and then I'll head to my assignment. As soon as I can, we'll find a little place, and I'll fly you out there."

"I know, but that's so long to wait," she whined. He loved Samantha. Really, he did, but he hated the whining when she didn't get her way. She was spoiled, her parents giving her and her sister, Susie, anything they wanted. The difference was Susie didn't act like a spoiled brat. She was a good kid.

"Baby, listen to me; the time will fly by. I have to do this, Sam. You know that. Mama needs my help, and I can't find anything that will make me good money around here."

"You could go to the oil fields like Richie and Gerald. They're making so much money, they're already buying their own houses."

"I'm happy for them," he said with exasperation, "but we've had this conversation. I don't want to work in the oil fields. My father died doing that work, and I won't put my mother through that." Sam stomped a stubborn foot, pulling on the sundress that showed way too much leg and boob for his liking.

"Fine, Bennie, but you know how lonely I get." Ben withheld any comments, just gathering his things as he dressed. At the door of the motel, he kissed her forehead, frustrated by her behavior and attitude.

"I'll be back soon." His gut told him that he probably wouldn't be back soon, but he watched as she sped out of the parking lot in her candy-apple red Mustang. A gift from her father. As it would turn out, she was right. He didn't go back soon. It would be nearly two years before he returned to get her, having finished Special Forces training. Now he was a Green Beret. He could return to her as one of the most elite soldiers in all the military with a paycheck reflecting that.

Samantha didn't answer her phone, so he went to her parents' home only to find her little sister, Susie. She didn't know where her sister was and asked him to stay, except he couldn't. Something about little Susie was different than when he'd seen her three years ago. She was taller, prettier, somehow more confident.

He searched half the night for Samantha, finally entering one of the many backwoods bars littering the bayous he called home, and there she was. Seated at the bar, her tongue down the throat of Richie Blanchard, her skirt hiked up nearly to her hips, his hands feeling his way around her. Calming his temper, he walked slowly toward the two when Samantha finally looked up.

"Bennie! What are you doing here?" she said, smiling and jumping off the stool into his arms. He pushed her back.

"I told you I was coming home," he said. "Richie. Nice to see you."

"Nice to see you, Ben. Sorry about this. Thought Sam told you we were engaged."

"Engaged? No, she didn't tell me that." He turned his gaze to Samantha, waiting for an explanation.

"Don't know what you want from me, Bennie..."

"Don't call me that. My name is Ben, Benjamin, or Blade."

"Blade?" she scoffed. "Whatever. You ran off to play toy soldier, and I was alone. A girl has needs." Blade nodded at the couple, noticing the apologetic look on Richie's face.

"Well, then. Good luck." Turning on his heels, he went back into the parking lot, only to run smack into Susie Doiron. "You followin' me, Susie Q?"

"N-no... I just... are you okay?" she asked.

"Will be," he said, side-stepping her. "See ya later, Susie Q. Take care." He watched her in his rear-view mirror, the neon lights of the old bar at her back as she lifted a small hand to wave at him. Something about that little wave made him want to turn around, but there was nothing for him back there. His future was forward, miles from this little speck of swamp.

"Time to make a new life."

OTHER BOOKS BY MARY KENNEDY YOU MIGHT ENJOY!

REAPER Security Series
Erin's' Hero
Lauren's Warrior
Lena's' Mountain
Sara's' Chance
Mary's Angel
Kari's Gargoyle
Rachelle's Savior
Adele's Heart
Tori's' Secret
Finding Lily
Montana Rules
Savannah Rain
Gray Skies
My First Choice
Three Wishes
Second Chances
One Day at a Time
When You Least Expect It
Missing Hearts
Trail of Love

Steel Patriots MC Series
Ghost – Book One
Doc – Book Two
Whiskey – Book Three
Zulu – Book Four
Gunner – Book Five
Tango – Book Six
Razor – Book Seven
Ace – Book Eight
Hawk and Eagle – Book Nine

My SEAL Boys (connections to the REAPER Series)
Ian
Noa
Carter
Lars
Trevor
Fitz
Chris
O'Hara

Strange Gifts Series
Dark Visions
Dark Medicine
Dark Flame

ABOUT THE AUTHOR

Mary Kennedy is the mother of two adult children, has an amazing son-in-law, and is grandmother to two beautiful grandsons. She works full-time at a job she loves, and writing is her creative outlet. She lives in Texas and enjoys traveling, reading, and cooking. Her passion for assisting veterans and veteran causes comes from a strong military family background. Mary loves to hear from her readers and encourages them to join her mailing list, as she'll keep you up-to-date on new releases at https://insatiableink.squarespace.com. You can also join her Facebook page at Insatiable Ink.

Dear Readers,

I love hearing from you and encourage you to visit my website Insatiable Ink. Leave me know your thoughts and ideas on new books or expanding on characters. It's also a safe space to give your own feelings, like those of the characters. I love reading about how you relate to the stories because as we all know, there's a little of each of them within us.

I look forward to hearing from you and hope you enjoy other books in my collections.

Explore... and enjoy!

www.ingramcontent.com/pod-product-compliance
Lightning Source LLC
Chambersburg PA
CBHW071511170626
46811CB00007B/2814